KARMA

All our chapters in just a second.

Luis Omar Herrera Prada

KARMA: ALL OUR CHAPTERS IN JUST A SECOND

© Luis Omar Herrera Prada

This novel was created with love, patience, and extensive rewriting. The original drafts were in Spanish, which I translated myself with some help from DeepL. I utilized AI tools, such as Grammarly and ChatGPT by OpenAI, to edit and enhance grammar, tone, and flow. ChatGPT generated images based on detailed descriptions of the characters that I provided. Any resemblance to real people or characters is purely coincidental, and no character is based on any specific individual.

Luis Omar Herrera Prada
www.herreraprada.com

I hope you enjoy this story in the plane to Phillipines!

Luis Omar Herrera P

CHAPTER ONE - THE INTERVIEW

Fairfax, Virginia. Prosperity Avenue. Uscis Field Office.

"Alright," the immigration officer says, adjusting her glasses. "So... let me get this straight. How many previous marriages have each of you had?"

"Three," they answer in perfect sync.

The officer blinks, pen hovering mid-air. "To each other?"

Jennifer nods. Sebastian shrugs.

- "Yes," she says softly.

- "Technically, yes," he adds.

The officer puts her pen down, leans back in her chair, and narrows her eyes. "Do either of you... have a sense of how insane that sounds?"

Jennifer smiles. Not a mocking smile, but one full of nostalgia and a quiet kind of madness—the kind you earn after surviving what they've survived.

Sebastian runs a hand through his hair. It's shorter now than it used to be, but the blonde still glows under the fluorescent light. He leans forward and rests his elbows on the desk.

"We thought you'd ask," he says.

The officer folds her arms. "Try me."

Jennifer glances at Sebastian. He nods. She inhales deeply and begins.

"It started in California. Santa Ana. I was the nanny. He was the golden boy."

Jennifer – Santa Ana, California – Thirteen Years Earlier

I didn't even want the job.

I applied to three families. The first didn't answer, and the second said no. The third—the Franz family—called me after five minutes. I took it as a sign from God. In hindsight, I think it was the devil playing a joke.

Franz was loud, British, and possibly drunk the day I arrived. He opened the door shirtless, holding a soccer ball and a baby in the same arm. "You must be Jennifer!" he shouted. "God, you're tiny. Are you sure you can handle twins?"

I almost turned around and left.

But then I saw the girls—two curly-haired chaos bombs in matching unicorn pajamas—and I smiled. I don't know why. I just did.

I moved into the guest house that same night. It was bigger than my parents 'apartment in Bogotá. It smelled like expensive laundry detergent and cinnamon. California light streamed through the windows like something out of a movie. I cried in the shower—quietly, so no one would hear.

The next morning, I met him.

Sebastian.

Blonde, tall, shirtless (of course), eating a bowl of cereal like he had nothing in the world to do but look beautiful and chew loudly.

He looked up at me, squinting. "You're the new nanny?"

I nodded.

"Cool. I'm Bas. Or Bastian. Or Sebas. Whatever you want."

I didn't understand half of what he said. I just nodded again.

He smiled, and it was— I mean, it wasn't a hot smile, not like the men in movies. But there was something in it. Mischief. Curiosity. Warmth. I knew that smile was going to be a problem.

I had no idea just how big.

For weeks, we barely spoke. Not because of distance. We lived meters apart. But I was quiet, and he didn't notice quiet girls unless they laughed too loud or wore something tight.

Sometimes we crossed paths in the gym. He always smelled like eucalyptus and chocolate. I hated that I noticed. I hated that I started timing my workouts just to be around him. I hated it even more when he stopped coming.

Other times, he'd join me when I took the girls to the park. He'd run laps around the soccer field while I sat in the grass, braiding little heads and telling stories about unicorns that cried glitter.

There was tension. Unspoken things. Glances too long to be innocent. Smiles that held just a second too long. But nothing happened.

Until one Thursday night.

The girls were finally asleep after a two-hour tantrum and a failed attempt at making arepas in a toaster oven. I was exhausted. My back ached. I smelled like applesauce and baby shampoo. I was halfway into my pajamas when I heard it.

Crying. Not a baby cry. A man's.

Muffled, frustrated, raw.

I stepped out of my room and followed the sound to the kitchen. The light was on. Books were spread all over the table. Highlighters, empty coffee cups, a half-eaten protein bar. And there he was.

Sebastian. Head in his hands. Shoulders shaking.

I froze. Something twisted in my chest.

I hadn't seen a man cry like that since Felipe.

Felipe.

The ghost in my brain. The voice that explained trade theory like it was poetry. The man I almost built a life with. The man who would've raised our child, who never knew he almost had one.

I didn't want to think about him. But he rushed in—like a wave. And then... something strange happened.

I didn't fall apart.

I stood taller.

I walked in quietly and sat down across from Sebastian. He didn't look up.

"Economía?" I asked.

His eyes lifted, red, glassy. "Yes," he sniffed. "It's… I don't get it. I'm failing."

I looked at the textbook. "Principles of Microeconomics. Chapter 5. Elasticity."

I nearly laughed. The irony was unbearable.

I pushed the book toward me and pointed at a formula. "Esto… is easy," I said softly. "Price elasticity is… how much people change their minds… when the price changes."

He blinked. "You know this?"

I nodded. "Is my degree. In Colombia."

His eyes widened. "Wait—you studied this?"

I gave a small smile. "Graduated. Top of my class."

He stared at me like I'd just appeared out of thin air. As if I'd been invisible all this time. I didn't blame him. I had made myself invisible. Easier that way. Safer.

But now? Now, I wanted him to see me.

I pulled the book closer. I picked up a pencil. And I began to explain. Slowly. Carefully. Like Felipe used to do for me. Every formula, every graph. My Spanish broke through the English, and sometimes I made mistakes. But Sebastian listened. Eyes wide. Head nodding.

He smiled when he finally got something. That smile again. And for the first time since I lost the baby, I felt useful. Not just needed—important.

We studied until past midnight. I don't know when he stopped crying. I just know when I got up to go, he grabbed my wrist gently.

"Thank you, Jen," he said. And he meant it.

That was the first time he said my name like it mattered.

Jennifer – That Night, Alone

When I finally made it back to my room, the girls were still asleep—one of them clutching a stuffed dinosaur, the other snoring softly with her mouth open.

I sat on the edge of my bed, still holding the pencil he gave me. My mind was loud. Too loud.

It felt strange—good, but strange—to be the one explaining. The one who knew. I had never realized how much I liked that role until it was mine.

With Felipe, I was always the one asking. The one learning. He would sit beside me in the university library, lean in, smell like rain and coffee, and whisper international trade theory into my ear like it was a secret meant only for me. He was brilliant. A little too old. A little too complicated. But brilliant. I loved him. Fully, completely.

He would have been the best father.

I never told him about the baby. Or the loss. I told myself it was to protect him. But sometimes I wonder if I was really protecting myself. If I had told him…, would I still be in Colombia? Would we be married? Would I be someone's mother now? The ache in my chest was familiar.

And now—this boy. Sebastian. Crying over elasticity and sunk costs. He was nothing like Felipe. And yet… I saw pieces of Felipe in him. But maybe worse—I saw pieces of Felipe in me, with him.

That scared me more!

He said he signed up for the class because someone told him it was easy. Said he was good at numbers, but this? This made no sense to him. And now, if he failed, he might lose the scholarship. And with it, the last threads of a dream he no longer truly believed in.

He told me, between graphs and equations, that when he was in the academy at Borussia Dortmund, all he thought about was playing in the World Cup and being like his father. Wearing the jersey and becoming the story. Now he was just trying to stay afloat.

He was only nineteen. Nineteen!

I hugged my knees to my chest and pressed my forehead to them. I didn't cry. Not tonight.

But I let myself imagine—just for a second—what would happen if I kept helping him. If I stayed close. If I became something more than the quiet girl in the background. I didn't know what that meant. I just knew I didn't want to disappear again.

Not this time.

CHAPTER TWO
– SEBASTIAN

Sebastian had a ball on his feet before he had shoes on.

That's how his mother used to tell the story, anyway. She'd say it with a smile, proud but tired. She had raised two sons who lived and breathed football, and one husband who never truly retired from it.

The Müller name was heavy in Germany. Heavy like trophies. Like expectations. His father had worn the number 9 jersey for the national team and scored in the World Cup. His face was on cereal boxes. His legs were in Adidas ads. His voice still called matches on TV.

Everyone expected greatness from Sebastian.

Or worse comparison.

He wasn't the first son. His older brother, Lukas, had been the prodigy. Stronger. Taller. Faster. The next Müller legend in the making. Until he wasn't.

Lukas broke his tibia during a brutal tackle in the UEFA U-19 Championship. A jump gone wrong. A mid-air collision. A leg snapped clean. A scream heard by every living room in Germany.

Sebastian was twelve. He watched it live.

Since that day, he has hated jumping. He never said it out loud. Never gave it a name. But when the ball went high, his chest tightened. His timing failed him. His mind froze. He trained for it. He tried. But it lingered. A shadow. A fear.

Lukas never recovered. Not really. He walked fine. He even coached. But he never stepped on the pitch the same way again. The shine left his eyes. He had no plan B.

Neither did their father. Jürgen Müller had been lucky—fast, aggressive, talented, and mostly injury-free. But he knew the sport could take everything in a second. He knew how fragile a career was.

So with Sebastian, he did something different. He gave him an escape hatch.

When the German press started calling Sebastian "a perfect blend of Busquets, Iniesta, and Messi"—when they said "Germany will be unstoppable with this Müller at full potential"—Jürgen panicked.

He saw the same lights forming around his youngest that had blinded his eldest. He called Franz.

Franz, his best friend from the Bundesliga days. Now living in California, raising half a dozen children, and working with sports networks. Franz had space. He had distance. And most of all, he didn't care about German hype.

"Send him here," Franz had said. "I'll give him freedom. And a gym membership."

So, Sebastian left.

At seventeen, he packed his boots, his doubts, and the legacy of a broken brother—and moved to Santa Ana. He got a soccer scholarship, a luxurious room in Franz's guesthouse, and just enough anonymity to breathe again.

He was good. Really good. Smart, fast, tireless. Not a 9 like his dad, not a 10 like Lukas—he was an 8. A midfield machine. Always moving, always thinking, connecting lines. Recovering. Attacking. Rebuilding. His lungs were better than his feet.

His weakness? The air. But on the ground, with the ball at his feet, he was poetry.

He was Felipe with a football.

Now he was failing microeconomics. He'd taken the class because someone told him it was easy. "For athletes," they said. "Just show up and pass the midterm."

Bullshit!

Now he was drowning in elasticity and marginal utility, crying like a child at the kitchen table.

He did not need the cash, but the ego, the opportunity. The scholarship was tied to grades. If he failed, he'd lose it. If he lost it, he might have to go back. Not to Germany. To a dream he no longer fully believed in. He didn't want to be Lukas. He didn't want to wake up at 25 wondering who the hell he was without a ball.

But plans didn't come naturally to Sebastian. The only future he ever pictured was made of stadiums and spotlights. Until she sat down across from him.

Jennifer. Jen. Quiet, soft-spoken, almost invisible—until she wasn't.

She had looked at his textbook like it was a novel. She had pointed to the formula like it was obvious. She said elasticity like it was a word that mattered. And when she talked, she stumbled between languages but never between ideas.

She was brilliant. And calm. And kind. And beautiful, but not the kind of beauty he usually noticed. It was the kind that grew in silence. The kind that surprised you. The kind you didn't see until it was right in front of you, helping you not fail your damn class.

And she saw him! Not the son of Jürgen. Not the kid with the press buzz. Not the athlete.

Just… Sebastian.

He hadn't realized how much he needed that.

He passed the exam. Barely. But he passed.

And it felt... weird. Like cheating. Like he had copied answers without knowing how. Except he did know. Sort of.

Everything he thought was impossible now sounded like her voice in his head: her soft accent turning graphs into stories, her hand pointing to formulas, her face focused, patient, lit by the kitchen light.

She was to economics what he was to the ball. And it shook him. How do you tell someone that?

How do you say, "I passed because of you," without sounding pathetic? How do you say, "You made me feel seen," when you've spent your whole life being watched?

She didn't even celebrate when he told her. Just smiled and said "Bien."

And maybe that was worse. Because he couldn't stop thinking about it. About her. About that night.

He had a list of girls he could call, could text, could disappear into. But Jennifer? She wasn't a "call." She wasn't a "hey, what are you doing tonight?" She was a jump.

And he didn't know how to jump.

He was still that kid frozen in the air, watching his brother fall. He wasn't afraid of failing. He was afraid of not knowing what to do after he didn't.

CHAPTER THREE
– JENNIFER

Santa Ana. Saturday Morning.

The girls were chasing butterflies. Literally.

Cora had one shoe on. Lila had grass in her hair. Both were screaming in Spanish and English and something in between, waving tiny nets they got from the dollar store like they were on safari.

Jennifer sat on the edge of a picnic blanket with her legs tucked under her. The sun was warm. The breeze smelled like sunscreen and waffles. It should've been a perfect morning.

But her mind was a mess. Sebastian. And Felipe. And her. She kept mixing them up in her thoughts—faces, voices, feelings. Sebastian had Felipe's quiet eyes, the way they softened when he listened. But more than that, he brought out in her what Felipe once did: this hunger to teach, care, and give. To make someone better. It scared her.

She hadn't felt useful like that in a long time.

She handed the girls their water bottles and looked up just as he appeared on the other side of the soccer field, running. His shirt was soaked, his blonde hair damp, and his stride determined.

And then, he saw her. It was like someone pressed slow motion. His feet stopped. His eyes locked on her. For a moment, he didn't move. He just watched. The world stopped totally at that time.

She turned to the side and smiled politely at two guys jogging shirtless nearby. They were college-age, friendly, and flirty. They said something in English she half-understood—something sweet. She laughed and waved.

Sebastian didn't move. He wasn't used to this feeling. Was it jealousy? Panic? Was this what a defender felt like when they realized the striker had already passed them? He felt out of place. And she had no idea.

Lucy, a girl from his econ class—one he'd casually hooked up with once or twice or more—ran by, recognized him, and stopped. "You, okay?" she asked.

He blinked. -"What?"

-"You look... weird. Like you saw a ghost."

He shrugged. -"Maybe I did."

-"You wanna walk? I was gonna grab something cold."

He nodded, barely listening. Minutes later, they were standing by a food truck. He bought two chocolate ice creams. But didn't offer her one.

Lucy looked at him. -"Okay... you're acting weird. I wanted to...."

-"I know," he said flatly and delayed, distracted.

She laughed nervously. "Well... I'm gonna head out."

He nodded, not even pretending to stop her. His brain was full. Heart racing. Muscles warm. He felt like he was about to play a final he hadn't trained for.

Jennifer was still at the park. One of the shirtless guys was leaving. She hugged him and said goodbye with a smile. And something inside Sebastian collapsed. The butterflies were not calm.

Then—screams. Not panic. Not fear. Just joy.

"¡Baaaaas!" The twins saw him and ran at full speed. Cora almost tripped. Lila dragged a butterfly net like a sword.

He bent down and caught both at once. They wrapped their arms around his neck.

And then, she appeared behind them. Running. Laughing. Wind in her hair. Cheeks pink from the sun.

"¡Gracias!" she said, breathless, as she caught up. "I thought they'd end up in the lake."

He smiled.

-"Are you okay?" she asked, noticing his expression.

He wasn't. He was all nerves and instincts and heat and confusion. But he nodded.

-"Yeah. I… I just wanted to say I did well on the exam."

Her eyes lit up. "Really?"

He scratched the back of his neck. "Yeah. And now I think maybe I should be an economist."

She laughed. "You'd be the first economist who actually knows how to play football. Every PhD program would kill for you."

He smiled, for real this time. "Hey, uh…" he hesitated. "Would you maybe… help me study tonight? There's this new chapter. It looks… intense."

She tried not to smile too fast. She had waited weeks for that excuse.

-"Sure," she said. "After dinner?"

He nodded. "After dinner."

The girls tugged at his hands. He let them lead him toward the swings. Jennifer stayed still for a moment, watching him go.

And for the first time, the confusion in her chest didn't feel like a warning. It felt like… a beginning.

CHAPTER FOUR
– FELIPE

They met in the back row of Room 306.

Technically, he was in the front, lecturing about trade agreements and capital flows. She was in the back, notebook open, eyes half-closed from the night before.

Jennifer was usually focused. Disciplined. But that semester, everything collapsed at once.

Her mother had been sick, her father had crashed the taxi, and her sister Paula was pregnant again. Money was tighter than ever. She worked nights at a bakery and slept maybe three hours a day.

She failed her first quiz. Missed two classes. Barely made it through midterms.

She had a boyfriend, a fellow student. Loud, overconfident, always pulling her into drama. One night, after another exhausting shift and a dozen unanswered messages, she finally texted him something simple on Facebook.

"Muah."

With a little heart emoji. She sent it without thinking. Only realized her mistake when she saw the name above it. Felipe. Her professor.

She froze. Her heart dropped.

She texted again immediately—"*Lo siento, error, no era para usted, perdón*"—but it was too late. There was no response.

In the next class, Felipe barely looked at her. She was mortified.

Her boyfriend shrugged it off. But Felipe's girlfriend, who, it turned out, was real, didn't.

The whole thing became gossip fuel. And Jennifer, who already felt like a mess, began to disappear from her own life.

Until one afternoon, she stumbled out of class, pale, on the verge of fainting. She sat down in the hallway, shaking. Her boyfriend didn't follow her.

Felipe did.

"Are you okay?" he asked, kneeling beside her. "Do you need water? Should I call someone?"

It was the first time he'd spoken to her directly since the message.

She nodded. He stayed beside her until her pulse slowed.

He never mentioned the text.

The next time was a Tuesday. She was rushing back from her nephew's baptism—her sister had insisted on doing it that morning so the godfather could attend, and the whole thing had been chaotic. Jennifer arrived at campus late, in heels, a too-tight dress, carrying a small gift bag with sugar-sticky fingers still clinging to her from a goodbye hug.

She tried to cross the plaza outside the lecture hall. Her heel snapped, and everything in her purse flew: lipstick, pens, old receipts, and a folded syllabus now smeared with caramel.

No one stopped except Felipe.

Jeans, gray sweater, no hesitation. He crouched down and helped her pick it all up.

No jokes. No comments. No judgment.

Just a quiet man, handing her back her things.

People saw. People talked. The next day, she was already the center of new rumors.

But Jennifer wasn't listening anymore.

That same Tuesday, after class, she went to the cafeteria, still wearing part of the baptism outfit, barefoot now in flats, her ankle sore.

It was Frijol Tuesday—legendary at the university. The rich and smoky beans were served on trays with rice, sweet plantains, and spicy arepa chips. She loved them. She never missed them.

She walked in, picked up her tray, and turned—just as Felipe stepped into the line.

Their eyes met.

Neither smiled. Neither waved.

But something passed between them.

A flicker. A shift. Like gravity had shifted half a centimeter to the left. They didn't say anything. They just sat at separate tables. Ate quietly and walked away, knowing that something had changed, without saying a word.

When the semester ended, she sent him an email asking to be his teaching assistant. He replied two days later.

"Why you?" he wrote. "You weren't exactly a star student."

She answered with the truth.

"Because I was drowning. And I know I'm better than what you saw."

A week later, his response came.

"Mondays and Thursdays. 4 pm. My office."

It started professionally. Lesson planning. Guidelines. Grading. Prep sessions.

Then came the coffee breaks. The small jokes. The silences that stretched too long. The way he started waiting for her opinion before finishing his thoughts.

She was twenty. Still a virgin. And very unaware of what she was feeling. She didn't fall in love with the professor. She fell in love with the man who opened up in those quiet hours—who admitted when he didn't know things, who shared his music, who made politics sound like stories and trade theory feel like magic. The kind of guy whose presence was there, even when he was not around, because you keep thinking about his sentences, his quotes, his faces. And that guy gives her space to express, to show the wings, and helps you fly safely. He has everything her actual boyfriend missed, and she felt that she fit with him perfectly in his arms and in his heart.

They lasted three years, in secret, in shadows, in rhythm.

She never planned it. Never chased it. But once it started, she couldn't imagine herself without it.

Two years in, she missed her period. She didn't panic. At first. But when the test showed two lines, her whole body went cold. She wanted to wait for the first ultrasound. She wanted to tell him when she had something real to show. She thought she had time.

She didn't.

Before the appointment came, she started bleeding. There was no dramatic scene. No trip to the hospital. Just a quiet, brutal night in her apartment, curled into herself, holding the test and thinking about what might've been.

She never told him, even though she wanted to. She almost did, but how do you tell someone they almost became a father without breaking something?

So, she buried it. Filed it under "never happened" and kept moving forward.

Eventually, the relationship ended the way some books do: with no real ending, just a final page.

She wanted more. He couldn't leave. She had outgrown the shadows. He asked her to stay.

She didn't.

She looked at the life they built and realized it was made of beautiful things that couldn't last. And then she left.

Now, years later, sitting under the California sun with twin girls playing at her feet, Jennifer still remembered him. Not with regret. With clarity. She had loved him. But she was no longer that girl in borrowed heels, sending hearts to the wrong man.

She had been broken. She had rebuilt herself. And maybe... just maybe... that was enough.

CHAPTER FIVE – AFTER DINNER

The house was quiet.

The kind of quiet that only comes after twin girls have finally fallen asleep, the dishes are done, and everyone has retreated to their corners of the night.

Jennifer stood by the kitchen sink, drying her hands. She could still smell bubble bath and arequipe. Her hair was pulled up. No makeup. Just her.

She looked at the clock.

9:04 p.m.

He hadn't forgotten. She was sure of it. He wasn't the kind of boy who forgot.

She walked to his room, notebook in hand, just in case. Sebastian opened the door before she knocked.

Like he'd been waiting.

"Hey," he said, stepping aside. "I made tea."

She smiled. "You drink tea?"

"Only when I'm pretending to be serious. Oh God, you want coffee?"

She stepped inside. The place smelled like cocoa and cologne. His notes were scattered on the table. Two mugs waited, one already half-full.

She sat across from him. There was a beat of silence.

He cleared his throat. "So… market structures."

She opened her notebook. "Do you know the difference between monopolistic and oligopolistic competition?"

He nodded slowly. "I know one of them sounds cooler."

She tried not to laugh. "Fair."

They began with diagrams—marginal costs, demand curves —graphs that used to feel like chaos now fell into place with her voice guiding him.

But something was different tonight. He wasn't just listening. He was watching her.

How her eyebrows moved when she concentrated. The way she pushed her hair back when it fell forward. The soft rhythm of her voice when she explained equilibrium like it was a love story between price and quantity. She asked him a question about collusion.

He didn't answer. He was still looking at her.

"Sebastian?"

"Hm?"

"Are you okay?"

He blinked. "Yeah. Just... I don't know. You're really good at this."

"At what? Economics?", she replied

"No. Well, yeah. That too. But I mean—at making things make sense. You talk and it's like... I don't know. Like the page, listens."

Jennifer looked down. A flush crept into her cheeks.

He kept going. "I passed that exam because of you," he said. "I couldn't stop hearing your voice in my head when I took it. You're like... you're like me, but with words instead of a ball."

She didn't say anything at first. And he didn't stop.

"I've had cameras on me since I was ten. People analyzing my steps, my shots, my stats, comparing me to my dad, my brother... but with you?" He paused. "You talk to me and I feel... seen. Like the person, not the story."

Now she was looking at him.

"Do you know how rare that is?" he asked.

She didn't answer. She didn't have to.

Outside, the wind picked up, and the trees rustled against the glass. Inside, something settled, and something else shifted.

He leaned back in his chair. "So... do you think if I keep passing these classes, I could maybe be an economist too?"

Jennifer grinned. "You'd be the most athletic one I've ever met."

He smiled.

Then, softer: "Would you keep helping me?"

Her eyes held his. "Yes."

There was a pause. A loaded one. The kind where something could happen—or not. And both choices would change everything.

Sebastian leaned forward. His voice dropped.

"Jen."

She inhaled.

"Yes?"

"I think I'm scared to jump."

She looked at him, carefully. "Why?" softly and intrigued.

"Because the last time someone jumped in my family, he never got up."

She nodded. She understood more than he knew.

"Then don't jump," she said calmly.

"What should I do?"

"Step," she whispered.

He reached out. Took her hand. Just her hand. And for that night, it was enough.

The next morning, the twins were eating cereal when Sebastian came into the kitchen. He had barely said good morning when Lila pointed a spoon at him.

"You like Jenny."

Cora giggled. "We saw you last night. You looked like you were gonna kiss her face!"

Jennifer almost dropped her coffee. Sebastian choked on air.

The girls howled with laughter.

Jennifer turned red and reached for their bowls. "Eat your cereal."

Cora sang under her breath: "Ba-aaaas and Jeeeen, sitting in a tree..."

Lila added: "K-I-S-S—"

"Enough!" Jennifer said, flustered but smiling.

Sebastian just grinned.

And in that moment, surrounded by spilled milk and sticky fingers, it felt like the beginning of something they didn't yet know how to name.

CHAPTER SIX – SEEN

Jennifer didn't believe in signs. She believed in facts, data, and probabilities. But that morning—after the study session, after the tea, after the step—she couldn't ignore the way the world felt... off. Not bad. Not chaotic. Just different. Like something had shifted an inch to the right. Like gravity had adjusted to make space for a new weight inside her.

The twins had gone full telenovela at breakfast. She hadn't expected that. Their tiny, teasing voices still echoed in her head.

"We saw you last night. You looked like you were gonna kiss her face!"

Sebastian had grinned.

Grinned!

And something in her heart had fluttered in a way she didn't want to admit. She spent the afternoon folding laundry, catching up on paperwork for the au pair program, reviewing visa renewals, and cleaning the fridge—anything to stay busy. Not to think. But she was thinking. Every time she looked at a dish, she saw his eyes. Every time she folded a shirt, she heard his voice.

"With you... I feel seen."

She didn't know what to do with that sentence. Because it was the exact thing she had longed to feel, once. Felipe had made her feel heard. But Sebastian? He made her feel seen. Not for her brain. Not for her role. Not for being the helpful one or the responsible one. Just... her. And it scared her more than she could say.

She went out to the park with the twins again. Sebastian wasn't there. A small part of her felt relief. Another part felt... disappointed. She sat on the bench, watching the girls chase pigeons, their giggles rising like little kites into the air. And she thought about something Felipe used to say:

"There are moments in life that split you in two—the person you were before, and the one who comes after."

Maybe last night had been one of those. But how could she trust herself to start again?

She had rebuilt her life once already. After leaving Colombia. After leaving Felipe. After losing the baby. Was she strong enough to risk it again? Or worse… *"querer"* again?

The sun was low when they walked home. The twins held her hands, sticky with melted popsicles and sidewalk chalk. She tucked them into bed an hour later, exhausted and clean and still humming the made-up "Bas and Jen" song.

She stood in the doorway for a moment after closing their bedroom door, holding the knob like an anchor. Then she turned and went out into the hall. Not to his door. Just… closer.

CHAPTER SEVEN
– FRANZ

Franz met Jürgen Müller in 1984. Playing in the Bundesliga, in August, during the first match of the season. Franz was a midfielder with too many opinions. Jürgen was a striker with too much t
alent.

They clashed immediately and badly. Fouls in training. Arguments in meetings. Shots fired—verbally and otherwise. But by winter, they were inseparable.

There was something about Jürgen's fire and Franz's instinct that just worked. Jürgen scored, and Franz created. Together, they built careers, reputations, and stories people still tell decades later.

Franz moved to the U.S. in the early '90s, just after the World Cup. He came to "help grow the game," as they said. The truth was, he needed a break from the press, the pressure, and the pile of ex-wives—you cannot even count them. He came to California and never left.

By the time he was fifty, he had children on three continents and a résumé that included TV punditry, minor league coaching, and a brief role in a soccer movie no one saw.

Then came Patricia. A Colombian architect, extremely elegant. She didn't care about his past or his fame. She had two rules: don't lie or waste time. He fell in love by accident. She was not sure of having kids, but she had twins.

By the time the twins were born, he was sixty-one. By then, he had learned how to shut up, listen, and be grateful. *"Si Señora"* became his favorite sentence. Patricia managed everything— house, routines, even his diet. But there was one thing she let him pretend to have a say in: The au pair.

The agency sent profiles—dozens—of young, smiling, eager women from all over the world. Franz was picking one from Austria when Patricia walked in, looked at the screen, and said, *"No. Esa. Jennifer. La chiquita de Bogotá.""* Franz raised an eyebrow.

"Why?"

"She looks like someone who's lived."

Franz leaned closer. The girl on the screen was thin and serious, not the smiley type. Her eyes were tired and sharp. He liked her instantly.

"Si señora," he said.

Jennifer arrived quietly. Polite. Efficient. She didn't ask for much. Took care of the twins like she'd known them forever. Cooked, cleaned, danced with them like a sister, and scolded them like a mother.

Franz started watching her like he watched games—carefully. Pattern recognition. Spatial awareness. She was smart, very smart. But she held things back. Pain, maybe, or stories she hadn't told yet. He started leaving the sports channel on when she was around. Started asking questions he knew she could answer. He wanted her to open up.

She didn't. Not right away.

But slowly, he saw it. The way her eyes lit up when she explained something. The way she sat taller when someone actually listened.

When Jürgen called about Sebastian, Franz didn't hesitate.

"Send him," he said. "I'll keep him out of trouble."

He had no idea that trouble would look like Jennifer.

But he didn't mind.

In fact... he helped it along. There were "accidental" schedule overlaps and shuffled park duties. Study hours suggested with a wink. Ice cream runs that conveniently left them alone. He watched them dance around each other like rookies with too much respect for the ball. He liked it. He liked them.

But he also knew the clock was ticking. One afternoon, he found Jennifer sitting on the porch, reading. He sat beside her with a sigh.

"You good?" he asked.

She looked up. Nodded.

"You like him."

She froze.

Franz smiled. "I'm old, not blind."

She hesitated. Then nodded again.

He leaned back in his chair and cracked his knuckles. "You know he's going back soon, right?"

Jennifer's face changed—just slightly.

Franz didn't push. He just looked at her the way he used to look at young players—those with too much potential and no idea what to do with it.

"Just take care of your heart, *niña,*" he said softly. "I'd hate to see it broken."

Jennifer blinked once.

Franz stood.

"Also, if you're going to fall in love with a footballer," he said over his shoulder, "at least make him pass his classes."

She laughed quietly. And Franz smiled all the way back to the kitchen.

CHAPTER EIGHT – FIRE IN HIS VEINS

Something had changed. He didn't know when exactly. Maybe that night with the tea. Maybe the moment she said "step." Maybe when she held his gaze after his confession and didn't flinch, all he knew was that his mind had stopped drifting. His body felt tighter, sharper, cleaner. His thoughts clicked into place like puzzle pieces, and for the first time in his life—

He was brilliant, not on the field. That had always been there.

But in the classroom. With books. With concepts. With graphs. With words.

All because she showed him how.

Sebastian, who used to pass barely, was now answering questions in class before the professor finished asking. His notes were color-coded, and his essays had footnotes. One of his economics instructors pulled him aside after a seminar and said, "I don't know what lit a fire under you, but keep it burning."

He just smiled and thought, Her name is Jennifer.

Then came the call.

The Uefa U-20 Championship.

The coach of the German national youth team had been watching Sebastian for months. They needed midfield strength, energy, and leadership. Sebastian had all three now.

He flew out a week later.

Jennifer took him to the airport. The twins cried. He promised to video call every other night. Jen nodded, trying to smile. He wanted to kiss her, but he didn't.

But his fingers lingered on hers a second too long when they said goodbye.

The tournament was fast. Brutal. Glorious.

Germany finished second. France took the trophy, powered by a golden generation of teenage monsters who would win the World Cup one day.

But Sebastian made a mark. Three goals. Every match played —Captain's armband in the semifinals and final. The cameras loved him. The press called him "The Engine." *"El Cerebro."*

But the most unexpected thing?

The celebration.

After his first goal—a bullet from outside the box—he ran to the sideline, dropped to one knee, and flapped his arms like a butterfly, then finished by spinning on the ground like a falling leaf.

The internet exploded.

"What was that?"

"Is he okay?"

"That was... kind of awesome?"

Within a week, it became a meme. Then a dance. Then a Fortnite emote mod.

Jennifer and Franz watched every match. Franz, with a beer in hand, shouted at the ref like it mattered. Jennifer, quiet at first, became more animated as the games went on. The twins wore face paint and called him "Capitán Bastian." When he scored, they screamed. When he celebrated, they laughed and tried to copy him on the carpet.

In a late-night video call, just after Germany beat Spain in the semifinal, Sebastian called them. Hair damp, voice hoarse, face lit with joy.

"Okay," he said, grinning. "Everyone keeps asking what the butterfly thing is."

Jennifer raised an eyebrow. "We were wondering that too."

He looked directly at her, then at the twins.

"It's you three," he said.

The girls gasped. Jennifer's heart skipped.

"Lila, because she always flaps her arms like that when she's excited. Cora, because she spins when she gets dizzy. And you"— his voice softened—"because you're the one who helped me fly."

She looked down, blinking fast. The girls screamed. "We're in Fortnite!"

After the final, he flew home to Germany for a short break. He saw his brother. Lukas was quieter now. Older in the eyes, still carrying what never healed. But proud. Honest. They talked long into the night about fear, recovery, and ambition. He saw his mother, who cried for fifteen minutes straight. He saw his father, who smiled like a man who had waited for this moment. Then came the dinner. Last night, before he'd fly back to California.

Everyone at the table. Stories. Laughter. Pictures. Childhood memories. Only happiness until Jürgen said it, calm, direct, and without drama:

"The club wants you, Sebastian."

He blinked. "Which club?"

Jürgen didn't smile.

"Dortmund."

Silence.

Then: "Professional contract. Full salary. Bonus for first-team appearances. They want you in camp after the summer. The press already knows. They're waiting for your confirmation."

Sebastian swallowed hard. He'd waited his whole life for this. But something in his chest... tightened. He nodded slowly. And said nothing else.

CHAPTER NINE – CHEERLEADER

Jennifer didn't know what to do with her hands during the matches. She clutched the remote.

Played with the corner of a pillow. Covered her eyes. Prayed, though she didn't realize it.

Franz shouted like he was in the stadium. The twins bounced around in pajamas with face paint smudged on their cheeks. But Jennifer… Jennifer suffered in silence.

Every time Sebastian touched the ball, her heart jumped. And something inside her hurt, though she didn't know why.

Because this wasn't her team. Because it wasn't Colombia. And yet…She was there. With him.

The first match, she watched in total stillness. The second, she dreamt about it afterward. The third… she lived it. When he scored that goal—from outside the box, full force—and ran straight to the camera, dropped to one knee, flapped his arms like a butterfly, then spun on the ground like a falling leaf…

She blinked. What are you doing, Sebastian?

Franz howled with laughter. "That boy's a star now! He's already gone viral!"

The twins mimicked the celebration on the rug, spinning until they fell over giggling. Jennifer just stared at the screen. She knew him well enough to know—it wasn't random.

By the fourth game, her hand was over her heart. By the fifth, she was standing, yelling directions like she could change the outcome from a living room.

In the final, her eyes were full. France was better. It was clear.

That team... that team would be a world champion one day. Germany fought hard. Sebastian wore the captain's band.

He ran like his lungs were limitless, organized the midfield like a conductor, screamed at defenders like a veteran, and picked up every teammate who went down. They lost. But he shone.

The final camera shot showed him hugging a teammate, exhausted, face unreadable but calm. Jennifer felt something quietly split open inside her.

Franz went to bed early. The girls were already dreaming of trophies. Jennifer sat alone on the couch in the dark, holding the remote like it was a life vest. She wanted to call him.

Not to say congratulations. To say I see you. Because he needed her. Because she needed him.
Maybe more than he knew. Maybe more than she knew.

She thought of something random: Captain Tsubasa. That anime her older sister used to watch with her first boyfriend, huddled on the couch after school. Jennifer had been too young to get it, but she remembered the story: the genius soccer boy, Tsubasa, and the quiet girl, always cheering him from the stands. Patty.

Always there. Always watching. Not part of the action—but essential anyway. Jennifer shook her head and whispered to herself, smiling a little: "I've become Patty."

And then— Breaking News.

Red banner. Bold letters. No warning.

"Borussia Dortmund pursuing U-20 captain after stellar tournament. Deal expected soon."

Below is a photo of Sebastian, a profile shot. A bandage is on his wrist, and the captain's armband is visible.

"The Prodigal Son Returns."

Jennifer froze. No thoughts. No breath. Just the screen.

Too much reality in thirty seconds.

CHAPTER TEN
– AIRPORT

The flight felt like it would never end.

Sebastian stared at the seatbelt sign like it was a clock stuck in the wrong time zone. The championship was over, the press was behind him, and his phone was drowning in messages from agents, journalists, Dortmund, ex-flings, and old friends he didn't remember giving his number to.

But none of them mattered.

None of them was her.

He stared out the window as the plane descended into California, thinking about her voice, her eyes, the way she looked the last night they studied, when he told her he was afraid to jump.

Now he was ready. For everything.

Jennifer couldn't breathe. She checked the arrivals board three times even though Franz had just said, *"Sí, niña, ya aterrizó."*

The twins were holding a handmade sign: "WELCOME BACK, CAPTAIN BUTTERFLY!"

Franz was eating trail mix like popcorn. Patricia stood calmly behind them, arms crossed, a smile forming. Jennifer... was shaking.

No more time. No more holding it in.

She thought about the way she watched every match. The way she broke down when she saw the news. The way she had replayed that spin, that celebration, that look in his eyes.

She wouldn't let it happen with silence if he was going to

leave again. She refused.

The doors slid open.

Sebastian stepped through with his duffel bag slung over his shoulder, his hoodie half-zipped, and his hair messier than usual. He looked exhausted—and perfect.

The moment their eyes met, time folded in on itself.

She didn't wait. She dropped her purse, ignored the twins' squeals, dodged a guy with a suitcase, and ran, straight to him.

He barely had time to exhale before she jumped into his arms and kissed him.

A kiss full of nerves, hope, fury, love, and everything she hadn't said.

Franz howled with laughter. The girls screamed and cheered. Patricia just smiled and whispered, *"Ay, se nos creció la familia..."*

Jennifer pulled back, breathless, face flushed.

"I'm proud of you," she said, fast. "And I'm sorry, but I had to do it like this because otherwise I wouldn't. And I know you have to go back, and I know I'll stay here and that's fine—well, no, it's not, but I'll deal with it. But I couldn't just stand there and wave at you like some distant ex-lover or—"

He cut her off with another kiss.

This time, slower. When they finally broke apart, he pressed his forehead to hers and whispered:

"I'm not going anywhere."

She blinked. "What?"

"I'm staying."

"Pero..."

"I already won on the field," he said, smiling. "Now I want to win somewhere else."

She stared at him, breath caught between shock and hope.

"And if the way to stay is marrying you?" he added. "Then I'll marry you tomorrow. Hell, tonight."

Jennifer opened her mouth. Closed it. Opened it again.

"I was just—how do you even—and I didn't mean for—"

He smiled wider. "I understood every word you said. Even in Spanish. Especially in Spanish."

She laughed. Cried. Bit her lip. And kissed him again.

Behind them, the girls started chanting, "*¡Beso! ¡Beso! ¡Beso!*"

Franz muttered, "About damn time."

Patricia crossed her arms, shook her head, and smiled with quiet pride.

"*Ay Dios!...*"

CHAPTER ELEVEN
– HOME

The car ride home was chaos—in the best way.

The twins fought over who got to sit next to Sebastian. Patricia handed out juice boxes like peace offerings. Franz was driving with the radio blasting and yelling every five minutes: "Captain Butterfly is BACK!"

Jennifer sat in the front, holding Sebastian's hand over the center console, occasionally turning to look at him, like she still didn't quite believe he was there.

And that he had stayed.

"*¿Estás seguro?*" she whispered at one point.

He nodded. "Completely."

The house had balloons—Patricia's idea. The girls had drawn welcome signs and stuck them on every wall. One had a heart with three stick figures: "Bas + Jen + Us."

Jennifer's cheeks hurt from smiling.

That night, they had pizza and wine. Sebastian told stories about the tournament, and the twins recited their version of his celebration, which was increasingly dramatic each time.

Franz slipped away for a phone call. When he returned, he handed Sebastian his phone.

"It's Jürgen."

Sebastian raised an eyebrow. "What?"

"Press won't leave him alone. Call him. Now. Fix it."

Sebastian sighed and stepped outside.

Jürgen's voice came through with no hello. Just:

"Are you insane?"

"Hi, Papa."

Jürgen: "Sebastian. Dortmund is offering a full contract. You could be in the Champions League next season. You walk away now, that window might close forever."

Sebastian leaned against the porch railing, breathing in the California night.

"I'm not walking away," he said. "I just chose a different kind of pitch."

Silence.

Then, quieter: "You really love her?"

"Yeah. And I'm not coming back without her."

More silence. Then the click of Jürgen hanging up.

Franz came out with two beers and handed one to him.

"He'll call back," Franz said. "He always does."

Inside, Jennifer was still smiling. But later, in bed, that smile faded. She stared at the ceiling, happy but unsettled. She should have slept like a baby. Instead, she dreamed of Felipe, books, classrooms, and a warmth that once held her together when everything else fell apart.

In the dream, he was watching her from a bench. Sebastian stood on a field in the distance, waving. Waiting. She walked toward one, then turned to the other. Then back and then froze. She woke up with a soft gasp. Why him, not Felipe? Why this? What part of me chooses?

Who do I love... and why?

Sebastian stirred beside her. Reached out, half asleep, and pulled her close. And that was the answer, at least for now.

The next morning, she said yes without blinking when he asked again—yes to everything: staying, marrying him, trying.

Sebastian started sketching out course plans. He would transfer programs, focus on economics, take it seriously, and build something long-term. Jennifer's visa time was running out fast.

Franz noticed. And didn't wait. He called a friend, an old connection from one of his corporate sponsorship days.

"Investment banking?" Jennifer said, stunned.

Franz winked. "You've survived this house. You'll survive Wall Street West."

A week later, she got the offer. It was for an entry-level role in research and strategy. It was not glamorous, but it was a foothold. It came with a work visa and a future.

That night, Jennifer stood in the living room, holding the job offer in one hand, Sebastian's hoodie in the other, and whispered to herself:

"I'm doing it."

No more shadows, nor hiding.

CHAPTER TWELVE
– REAL TALK

The night felt too quiet. They had dinner with the girls, laughed, watched cartoons, and talked about wedding colors (Cora insisted on purple, Lila on glitter). Everything felt perfect.

Until it didn't. Until the house was quiet again. Too quiet.

Sebastian and Jennifer sat on the guesthouse floor, backs against the couch. Two mugs of tea sat untouched. He hadn't looked at her directly in minutes.

She noticed. "What's wrong?" she asked gently.

He breathed in. Then out. Then again.

"I don't want to hurt you," he said.

She turned toward him. "Why would you?"

"Because I still don't know who I am without a ball at my feet. Because sometimes I feel like I'm chasing a version of myself that doesn't exist yet. Because... maybe you know me better than I know you."

She swallowed hard.

"And I don't want to be the guy you chose because you've already lost too much," he added. "I want to be someone you choose freely. Not someone who came in and filled a silence."

Jennifer looked down. Her hands trembled slightly.

Then she nodded and said, "I have to tell you something."

Sebastian stayed quiet.

So she told him about Felipe, about being twenty and falling in love with someone she shouldn't have. About being brilliant but broken. About the baby and the loss. The way she left. The silence she chose instead of pain. She said it all, slowly, carefully, and honestly. She didn't cry. When she finished, he didn't say anything right away. Just reached for her hand and held it tightly.

"I'm not afraid of your past," he said.

"But you should know it," she replied. "Because I can't promise I'm not carrying parts of it still."

He touched her cheek gently. "I'm carrying mine too."

They sat in silence for a long time. Then she said the thing that surprised even herself.

"I think you should go."

He turned sharply. "What?"

"To Europe. To play."

"No, Jen, I told you, I want to build this life. With you. Study. Be here—"

"And you can. But you were born for that field, Sebastian. You don't have to choose between football and me."

"I'm not going without you."

She smiled, tired but real. "You don't have to. We find a way. But promise me something?"

"Anything."

"Don't stay small for me. I won't let you."

The next morning, his phone buzzed with two offers: Arsenal and Chelsea. London was knocking. And this time, he had a say in how the story would go. He looked at Jennifer across the breakfast table, hair in a bun, glasses slightly crooked, reading The Financial Times with a highlighter. His heart squeezed.

"I'll go," he said aloud.

She looked up.

"If I can study economics while I play," he continued. "And if we live together. In London."

She blinked. Then smiled.

"Deal."

They had two weeks before preseason. Two weeks to plan a wedding. Two weeks to start a future. Two weeks to figure out how to fly. Together.

CHAPTER THIRTEEN – THE HOUSE THAT HELD THEM

The sun was high and bright over Santa Ana the day they got married.

No cathedral. No altar. No strings quartet. Just a courthouse, a city seal on the wall, and the people who mattered most.

Jennifer wore a pale blue dress that danced when she walked. Her hair was half-up, and her lips trembled with nervous smiles. Sebastian wore a navy button-down shirt with rolled sleeves and too-clean shoes.

Patricia brought flowers—tiny white roses tied with a blue ribbon. The twins wore mismatched socks and wide grins. Franz wore sunglasses inside and muttered something about allergies.

The ceremony was fast. The vows were improvised.

Jennifer's voice cracked. Sebastian's hands shook.

But when he slipped the ring onto her finger, and she onto his, everything stilled.

There was no choir. No cameras.

Just two young people saying yes out loud.

The celebration? In-N-Out. Of course, what else do you expect? (You, dear reader, may predict what is coming, for sure)

Sebastian dreamed of burgers, fries, strawberry milkshakes, and two six-year-old flower girls spilling ketchup on their white shirts.

They took selfies with greasy fingers. They fed each other fries.

Franz demanded a picture and said, "This one's going in my will."

At one point, Sebastian looked at Jennifer mid-bite and whispered, "We did it."

She smiled, cheeks full of food. And said, "We really did, and badly"

The next day, the house was filled with boxes. Luggage was stacked by the door. Little hearts drawn in Sharpie on a suitcase: "Don't forget us!"

Inside, everything felt different. Clean. Complete.

Jennifer stood in the middle of the living room, soaking it in— the couch where she cried that first week, the kitchen where she explained elasticity, the hallway where she first saw Sebastian without a shirt, and the place where she forgot her English, any other word, and some air more than once.

Every corner held a version of her. Sebastian came down the stairs with a final bag and dropped it with a sigh.

"They fit."

Patricia raised an eyebrow. "I organized them for you last night. Of course, they fit." Franz grunted. "You'd better come back famous. I've got money on you now."

Sebastian smirked. "That explains the pressure."

The girls came in holding a glittery poster that read, "London: BE READY FOR BUTTERFLY MAN AND JEN!"

Lila handed Jennifer a small box. Inside, a gold plastic ring: "It's for your wedding. Just in case you don't get a real one."

Jennifer laughed. Then cried. Then laughed again.

Cora hugged Sebastian's leg and whispered, "Don't forget to fly. I am your fan number 1."

He knelt down and pulled both of them close. "Never."

Then came the hard part. Franz stepped forward and held out his hand. Sebastian ignored it completely and hugged him —a real hug—the kind that says, "You changed my life, and I probably won't say it out loud, so here it is." Franz swallowed hard.

"You're a good man," he muttered.

Then turned to Jennifer.

"Tú también, niña."

She hugged him, tighter than she expected. *"Gracias por todo. Por más de lo que sé decir."*

He looked at them both. "Go. Build something."

Then added, dry as ever: "And don't name your first kid Franz. That would be cruel.". Franz went to bring the car.

Patricia approached quietly. Jennifer melted into her arms like a daughter who finally found the kind of mother she needed.

They didn't speak. They didn't need to. When they pulled apart, Patricia looked her in the eye and said:

"Recuerda quién eres. A dónde vas. Pero también de dónde saliste."

Jennifer nodded. *"Siempre."*

Outside, the car honked. The world was waiting. Sebastian took her hand. Jennifer squeezed it.

They turned, stepped out, and walked toward the future. The door closed behind them.

But not the chapter. Never the chapter. No yet, at least.

CHAPTER FOURTEEN – HOMECOMING

Franz got the family van, "for space", he said. It was planned, but otherwise it would seem suspicious.

When Sebas and Jenn thought the drama was over, Franz said: "I need to be honest, I talked to some friends. They upgraded your flight to a charter plane parked in John Wayne Airport".

In the van, "London first," Franz said casually. "Quick stop, you get some meal. Then you meet Jürgen and head to Chelsea."

Jennifer nodded, adjusting the girls 'carry-ons. Sebastian looked suspiciously calm.

It wasn't until they were 30 minutes from Bogotá's airport that Jennifer realized something wasn't right.

"Wait," she said, staring out the window. "That's not London."

Sebastian smiled. He knew what was happening.

"We're going to Colombia," he said

Jennifer blinked. "What?"

Franz said, "I'm old, not boring," when he told me he spoke to the club.

Sebastian leaned in.

"We thought… maybe it was time you got your own parade. Two weeks. First Bogotá. Then… you'll see."

Jennifer covered her mouth with her hands.

Bogotá

The arrival in Bogotá was chaos and magic.

Jennifer's entire family was waiting—her mom was crying,

her dad was holding a sign that said, "Welcome Home *Profesora*," and her sisters were loud and chaotic, which is exactly how she remembered them.

Sebastian held her hand through it all.

They stayed in Jennifer's childhood apartment for the first week—tight quarters, laughter in every room, late-night arepas, and impromptu salsa in the living room. Bastian tried dancing and nearly twisted his knee. Everyone loved him instantly.

Jennifer beamed like she hadn't in years.

One day, she took Sebastian to her university. He wore sunglasses and a hoodie, trying to blend in. It didn't work. Students kept asking if he was "that guy from the butterfly dance."

Jennifer rolled her eyes and walked faster. When they reached the economics building, her heart started racing, and he noticed.

"You okay?"

"Yeah. Just... this was my place," she said softly.

They reached the hallway. She glanced toward that office. The door was closed. She hesitated. Relief.

A secretary passed and caught her eye. "Oh, *Profesora* González! Did you hear? *El profesor* Felipe Santos went to Chicago. PhD. Finally!"

Jennifer froze. "Thank you," she said, almost inaudible.

Sebastian leaned closer. "Was that him?"

She nodded.

They walked past the door anyway.

Sebastian stopped in front of it. Looked at the nameplate. Then at her.

"You'd look good with your name on one of these."

She gave him a half-smile. "Too many ghosts."

He touched her hand. "Then let's make new ones."

Colombia

The second week was pure magic.

They went to the Valle del Cocora, walked among towering

wax palms and butterflies. Jennifer and Sebastian rode horses and laughed like children.

In Medellín, they took cable cars up the mountains and danced in Plaza Botero.

In Santa Marta, they sat on the sand at night, just the two of them, watching the waves.

"Colombia's insane," Sebastian whispered.

Jennifer leaned on his shoulder. "In a good way?"

"The best way."

One night, he called his mom. Jennifer sat beside him, half-asleep on the hotel bed. He spoke in German first and then switched to English for her.

"She's not just from Bogotá, you know," he said into the phone. "She's the whole country."

Jennifer blinked.

"She's got the strength of the Andes," he said. "The fire of Medellín. The softness of the Caribbean. The patience of the coffee valleys."

He paused, then smiled. "Mom, I think I picked the right Colombian."

Jennifer raised an eyebrow. "Think?"

He grinned. "Well… maybe the best one picked me."

CHAPTER FIFTEEN – LA ÚLTIMA AREPA

The final morning in Bogotá smelled like café con leche and farewell.

Jennifer's mother had been up since 5 a.m., preparing a breakfast that could feed an entire battalion: *calentado, pericos, almojábanas, arepas, jugo de mora.* Everything Jennifer ever loved was on the table.

All her sisters were there. Even Daniela, who had magically reappeared after months "exploring" Peru and brought back mysterious earrings for Jenn and a story about sleeping in a hammock with a monkey. Paula had her four kids in matching shirts, running circles around the table. Adela, quieter than the rest, handed Jennifer a small rosary. *"No es para rezar,"* she whispered. *"Es para recordarte que no estás sola."*

Jennifer hugged her tightly.

They didn't cry, not in public. But they all held her like they wouldn't get another chance.

Sebastian wore jeans, a black tee, and—causing total chaos in the room—a Millonarios jersey. Jennifer's uncles practically lifted him on their shoulders.

The press had gotten wind of his visit days ago, but that jersey turned everything into a firestorm. Cristian, Jenn's favorite cousin, posted a picture on Instagram, and the media boomed with rumors.

"La joya alemana ahora es embajador de Millonarios," joked one anchor.

Another headline flashed:

"Future star? Chelsea or Bogotá?"

"Sebastian Müller: *nuevo ídolo capitalino?*"

Colombian media even contacted Franz in California, and Franz didn't help. He answered one journalist's call from Santa Ana with:

"He loved the stadium, Bogotá, and Millonarios have too much history. And the empanadas. I don't know, maybe it's destiny."

Jennifer rolled her eyes. "Franz…"

Later, in a FaceTime call with the couple, Franz just winked. "It's good PR." Said.

At the airport, the chaos exploded. Two reporters popped out with mics and cameras as they walked toward security.

"Sebastian! Is it true you're signing with Millonarios?" "Are you staying in Colombia?"

"Who's your girlfriend?"

He smiled calmly. Jennifer froze.

Then he reached for her hand and pulled her close.

"She's not my girlfriend," he said into the mic, turning toward her.

"She's my wife."

Click. Flash. Boom. Just like that, it was on every screen in the terminal.

Jennifer looked radiant. Strong. Untouchable.

She didn't flinch. She stood beside him like she'd always been meant to.

Thousands of miles away, in a dorm apartment in Chicago, Felipe sat grading papers with the Colombian news channel humming in the background. He looked up just in time to catch the footage. There she was.

Jennifer. Hair longer. Smile brighter.

He leaned back in his chair and turned the volume up slightly. He saw Sebastian take her hand. Saw the camera's flash.

And he smiled. Not bitterly. Not sadly.

Just… smiled.

CHAPTER SIXTEEN – A DIFFERENT GAME

London was nothing like California. And nothing like Bogotá.

It was grayer. Faster. Colder in spirit, even when the weather wasn't. The buses were red, the sky permanently white, and people moved like they were being chased, never looking you in the eye.

Jennifer adjusted faster than she expected.

Something about the rhythm suited her. The Tube initially made her anxious, but by week two, she was navigating like a native. She started her first courses at LSE—Development Economics. Her mind came alive again.

On the other hand, Sebastian felt like a well-dressed tourist with access.

Chelsea had signed him, yes. Social media followed him. Training sessions were intense. But first-team minutes?
Rare.

Most of his time was spent in the reserves. Waiting, watching, and grinding.

And back at home... that started to eat away at both of them.

Their first fight was over a coffee mug.

Jennifer had barely slept. She had a deadline and two lectures, so she spent the night lost in poverty models and regression outputs. Sebastian used her favorite mug—the blue one with the tiny chips on the handle.

She snapped. "It's not the mug!"

He froze. "Then what is it?"

"It's everything! You're here, training, eating, sleeping, and

I'm barely hanging on!"

He stared at her, hurt. And then quietly asked, "Is that what you think of me?"

Silence.

She regretted it instantly. But didn't say it.

The arguments weren't constant but came more often than either liked.

About routines, or schedules. Misunderstandings between exhaustion and expectation.

He didn't always understand why she needed so much control or attention. She couldn't understand how he remained calm when nothing seemed certain.

But every night, they fell asleep holding hands. That part didn't change.

A month after arriving, the club offered something unexpected.

"We like that you're studying," the director said. "It makes you marketable. But... But not economics."

The team and a tech sponsor proposed a new plan: they'd cover a full degree in Data Science, with a focus on sports performance and tactical modeling.

Jennifer lit up when she heard it. Sebastian didn't.

"Feels like a detour," he said later that night. "I wanted to study economics... because of you."

Jennifer smiled softly.

"Maybe the point isn't what you study. Maybe it's that you're building something that lasts beyond the game."

He stared at her. The next day, he said yes.

One random Tuesday night, everything changed.

They called him up for a first-team match. Five minutes left. Tied score.

He stepped onto the pitch. Four touches. One assist. Victory.

Twitter exploded.

"The German whisperer."

"Müller Jr: one to watch."

Jennifer watched from the top row of the stadium,

surrounded by cold air and drunk fans.
She didn't scream. She just proudly smiled.

CHAPTER SEVENTEEN – LONDON LIFE

London had stopped feeling temporary.

They had favorite places now—the small Lebanese spot on Holloway Road, where Jennifer always ordered too much; the secondhand bookstore near Farringdon, where Sebastian found a signed copy of Moneyball; and Tesco, where the twins once FaceTimed them and shouted, "Buy snacks for us, it's bedtime!"

Life wasn't glamorous, but it was theirs.

Jennifer had finished her first term at LSE with distinction. She joined a research group focused on gender inequality and migration policy. This experience lit something in her— something that made her want to speak up more and stand taller.

Sebastian trained. A lot. More than he ever had.

And slowly, surely, it paid off.

His name started appearing in more lineups, first in the League Cup and then in the Premier League. He never played full matches, but he changed things when he stepped on the pitch.

He was quick, smart, and ruthless with the ball. The fans noticed. The staff noticed.

One day after training, the coach handed him a packet.

Flight info. Kit numbers. Champions League group stage. Away match in Portugal.

"You're in," the coach said. "Don't freeze."

That night, Jennifer found him sitting on the floor of their apartment, staring at the document like it was an invitation to another planet.

She crouched beside him. "You okay?"

He looked up, dazed. "Champions."

She grinned. "Butterfly man made it."

He laughed, pulled her into his lap, and whispered: "You made me." They celebrated with wine and takeout.

They danced barefoot in the kitchen. She wore his shirt. He kissed her shoulder like it was the first time.

At one point, she stopped and looked at him. "We're really doing it," she said.

He nodded. "And I don't want to stop."

When he boarded the plane for Portugal days later, press cameras flashed in his face.

One photo made the cover of a German sports magazine: "Sebastian Müller: The Next Legacy?"

Jennifer watched the live feed from their living room, wearing one of his old training jackets.

She wasn't nervous. Not anymore. She knew who he was now.

And more importantly, she knew who she was next to him.

CHAPTER EIGHTEEN
– THE HEIGHTS

The lights in the stadium didn't blink.

They blazed.

It was like stepping into a planet made entirely of breathless anticipation—thousands of voices, flags, and smoke. The Champions League anthem was playing as if God himself had composed it.

Sebastian stood on the edge of the pitch in Portugal, boots tied tighter than usual, heart pounding in a steady sync with the roar around him.

He was on the bench, of course. He wasn't a starter yet. But he was there.

In the lineup. In uniform. And that meant everything.

The match began tense. Two yellow cards were shown in the first twenty minutes. Chelsea scored first, and the home team retaliated furiously.

In the 65th minute, the coach turned to him.

"Warm up."

His legs moved before his mind caught up. Seventy-fourth minute. The board lit up: #27 in.

Debut (Jürgen, his dad was #9; Lukas, his older brother, played with #18, so he was #27).

Real. Alive.

He stepped onto the field with every nerve on fire. The grass felt different. The sky looked closer. And everything inside him quieted to one idea:

Don't waste it.

At home in London, Jennifer had planned to watch alone.

She ended up inviting two classmates over, and then Patricia called. The girls FaceTimed from California, yelling, *"¡Vamos, Capitán Mariposa!"* into the phone until the WiFi cut out.

She smiled as the camera zoomed in on him entering the field.

Hair is slightly longer now. Jaw tighter. Shoulders broader. He didn't look like the boy she met with an open textbook and a gym bag anymore. He looked like himself.

He didn't score that night. But he played well. Really well.

He won tackles. Built pressure. Almost assisted a second goal.

When the final whistle blew—Chelsea 2, Porto 1—he walked off the pitch soaked in sweat and adrenaline. And pride.

The press circled immediately. German papers called him "disciplined and elegant."

English commentators said: "There's something about this Müller. Reminds me of someone."

He called Jennifer from the tunnel. She answered immediately.

"Hi."

He smiled, breathless. "Did I look good?"

She laughed. "You looked like you were born for it."

He didn't speak for a moment.

Then said, softer: "I wanted to look like I belonged to you."

Two days later: The call…

The German National Team Senior squad. International break. Their next friendly? Colombia (I hope you guessed, dear reader…).

Jennifer dropped her spoon into the sink when he told her.

"What?" she blinked.

"In Madrid. End of next month. I'm on the list. I might not play, but—" He was practically bouncing. "Colombia, Jen!"

She didn't know whether to laugh or panic. He kissed her forehead. "We'll go together."

Over the next few months, life turned fast.

Sebastian was no longer "just the new guy." He got minutes, headlines, brand offers, and autograph requests, and tons of teens did his dance on TikTok again.

Jennifer smiled through it all. But she was also watching. Watching how people looked at her.

How suddenly, she wasn't the smart Colombian economist at LSE. She was "his wife." His shadow. His plus-one.

He started flying her out for matches. Rome. Munich. Seville.

They kissed under foreign skies. Made love in hotels with marble bathrooms and balconies.
Laughed over wine and pasta. Took pictures she never posted. She felt part of something larger. But also smaller. Because something was starting to pull them apart... gently.

Not violently. Not yet. Just softly. Like a string unraveling in slow motion.

She didn't tell him that on her way back from Seville, someone at the airport asked if she was "his assistant." She didn't tell him that sometimes she practiced saying "my name is Jennifer" in her head before meetings, as if she were forgetting herself. And she didn't tell him how it felt watching him shine, knowing she was proud of him—yes, so proud—but also unsure of where she fit in the picture.

They still held hands. Still cooked together when they could. Still shared dreams. But sometimes, she'd wake up and find herself staring at the ceiling, wondering: What happens if he outgrows me? What happens if I outgrow this?

None of those questions had answers yet. And neither of them was ready to ask them out loud. Not yet.

CHAPTER NINETEEN – CRACKS IN THE CANVAS

The day of the match was surreal.

Germany vs. Colombia.

Madrid. Friendly.

But there was nothing "friendly" about what Jennifer felt.

She wore neutral colors. Not the yellow, not the white.

She sat in the VIP section, still and anxious. Her fingers curled around the coffee cup in her lap like it was the only solid thing in the world.

She had grown up with Colombia in her blood.

The anthem still made her tear up.

But now, her husband was on the other side of the pitch. Lacing up his boots, wearing Germany's colors and looking proud, focused, and brilliant.

She didn't know who to root for.

The match was tight. Colombia scored first—an early header (#9 Falcao -of course-). The fans behind her roared. Her heart jumped. She almost clapped. Almost.

Sebastian entered in the 62nd minute.

Jennifer's hands trembled slightly.

He ran with intent, passed clean, cut lines like a scalpel. And in the 89th minute, when Colombia thought they had it—

He scored. A perfect strike. Right into the corner. The stadium gasped.

He didn't celebrate wildly. He just turned, found the VIP box with his eyes, and lifted one finger. One. Back at the hotel, they met up in the suite. She had changed into leggings and a hoodie, hair wet from a quick shower.

He was buzzing, still in training pants, his phone blowing up. "You saw it?"

"Of course," she said, half-smiling. "I always do."

He leaned in for a kiss, but she stepped away, pulling a towel off her hair.

He laughed. "You mad I scored against your team?"

"No," she said. "I'm proud. You were incredible."

"Then why the face?"

He smirked. "Because tonight, someone's sleeping on the couch."

Jennifer froze. He meant it as a joke. She knew that.

But it hit somewhere raw. "That's not funny."

His smile faltered. "Jen, I—"

"I'm tired, Bastian."

Silence.

A kind they hadn't known in a while.

Things stopped being magical after that. Not immediately. Not loudly. But enough.

He had back-to-back matches. She had midterm exams and faculty reviews.

They saw each other in passing. Touched less. Spoke less. And then came the email.

Subject: "Support Request – Job Market Presentation"

From LSE's department chair. A brief, formal note:

"We have a candidate presenting next month from the University of Chicago. His name is Felipe Santos. We noticed you share nationality and field. Would you be willing to assist him during his visit and help him navigate LSE?"

Jennifer stared at the screen. Her coffee went cold.

Felipe. Presenting at her university, in her building, in her life.

She hadn't heard his voice in years and hadn't seen him since… everything. The faculty had no idea, of course. To them, it was a logical connection—a kind gesture.

To Jennifer, it was like being hit from behind. The past had returned—uninvited. And she wasn't ready.

Maybe she didn't tell Sebastian right away because she didn't know how. Perhaps because they barely had time to sit at the same table anymore. Maybe because, deep down, she was afraid of how she might sound—nervous, shaken, uncertain—all the things she hadn't been in years.

So, she replied to the department chair with a short, professional "yes."

She would help. She would manage because that's what she did. How? Humm..

A week later, they finally had dinner together—an authentic dinner. At home. Pasta, salad, and wine. She lit candles. Tried. He looked at his phone three times before the salad was finished. She let it go until she couldn't.

"I need to tell you something," she said, not looking up.

He set his fork down.

"I'm helping someone at LSE with a presentation. He's from Colombia. Economics. His name is… Felipe."

He blinked. Then again.

"The Felipe?" he asked. "Felipe Felipe?"

She nodded once. He leaned back.

"You're serious?"

"He's just visiting. Presenting his job market paper. I was assigned to help."

"Assigned."

His voice wasn't angry. But it wasn't neutral either.

She stayed quiet.

"So, you said yes?" he finally asked.

"I didn't think I could say no."

He nodded. Slowly.

And didn't touch the wine for the rest of the meal.

In the days that followed, they became polite.

The kind of politeness that sounds like distance disguised as respect.

She left earlier. He came home later. She worked more at the

library. He booked extra training hours. They stopped dancing in the kitchen. Stopped falling asleep in each other's arms.
They still kissed, but short, efficient.

The night before Felipe's talk, Jennifer stayed up late re-reading the abstract of his paper. It was brilliant. Of course.

Her heart raced as she read his name. She imagined how he'd smile when he walked into the faculty lounge, smooth and sharp, just like always. She hated that she still remembered what his voice sounded like. And she hated that she hadn't told Sebastian how that made her feel.

Sebastian, meanwhile, had been on fire. Two goals in three weeks. A Nike feature. Endless press.

His phone buzzed like a heartbeat. He was everywhere. But not with her. And he knew it. He felt it. He just didn't know what to say

One night, after coming home from a sponsor dinner, he found her asleep on the couch, laptop open, her hair messy, glasses still on.

He stood there for a long moment. Watching her. Wondering what version of her he knew now. And who she became when he wasn't looking. He wanted to wake her up. To tell her he missed her. That he hated this silence. That he didn't want to be this kind of couple.

But instead, he walked to the bedroom alone. Closed the door behind him. And didn't sleep.

CHAPTER TWENTY – ECHOES

Felipe entered the room like time hadn't passed. Black shirt. Hair is a little shorter. Same smile. Wise, penetrating glance.

Jennifer stood by the faculty lounge table, holding a coffee tray. He smiled.

"Jen," he said, softly and kindly. "You're still the person who lights up any room." It was casual. Polite. But it broke something.

She blinked. Took a deep breath. "Welcome to London." They spoke like colleagues. Discussed the seminar, the audience, and the format.

But under her voice ran every memory. The late nights that whispered "I love you". The miscarriage. The pain. The quiet goodbye.

She thought she had moved on. And maybe she had. But memories didn't need permission to rise.

That night, she lay beside Sebastian, staring at the ceiling. She could hear him breathe. Steady. Calm. Asleep. She wasn't.

Her mind kept switching back and forth—then and now. Felipe and Sebastian. Passion and distance. Then she stopped trying to compare.

Because the truth was worse, she wasn't feeling much at all anymore.

Just... numb.

Sebastian didn't notice at first. He thought things would bounce back. One more game. One more good night. One more little reset. But it didn't.

She was quieter. Colder. Careful.

She started leaving sticky notes: Have a good day, *mi amor*. He replied with nothing.

One night, she said she wasn't coming to his match. He nodded. Didn't ask why. That was when she knew.

The thought of divorce didn't come as a thunderclap. It came like fog. Silent. Creeping. Eventually all-consuming. And when she sat with it long enough, it made sense.

She remembered what Felipe once told her, back when she cried in his office about not being enough:

"Sometimes we meet someone perfect for us. But only for who we were then. Not for who we're becoming."

She hadn't understood it back then. Now she did. Now it was her turn to say it.

The night she packed, she didn't cry. She folded everything slowly. She left her wedding ring on the table next to all her paperwork for divorce, which she had signed.

She left a handwritten note in careful print—because her hand was shaking too much to use cursive.

"Bastian,

I love you. But I don't think I'm supposed to keep you.

You need to fly. And I'm afraid I became the sky you can't lift off from.

I know what it means to be the dream that holds someone down.

I won't be that for you.

You've already made it. Now it's time to go even further.

I'll be proud of you always.

—Jennifer"

She booked a red-eye to Bogotá. No goodbye. No final kiss. Just air and memories.

When Sebastian woke up...

She was gone.

And he didn't realize how far until it was too late.

He finished the divorce paperwork as soon as he could.

CHAPTER TWENTY-ONE – THE ASHES

Bogotá

Bogotá felt… different.

Not because the city had changed, but because she had.

Jennifer didn't tell anyone she was coming. She just appeared at her parents 'door, suitcase in hand, quiet eyes, and a body that carried months of silence.

Her mother cried softly. Her father hugged her tightly than he ever had.

She didn't explain much. Just said she needed time. That was enough.

She fell into a rhythm—early mornings, helping with errands, taking her dad to medical checkups, reorganizing old drawers, watering plants, cooking lunches like she used to with her sisters. And most of all, she stayed away from everything that reminded her of London.

Especially football.

She stopped watching it. Stopped reading headlines. Didn't turn on the TV when the matches were on. She didn't even go to the stadium with her father and cousins—something sacred once.

That part of her life had been erased, just gone.

London

Meanwhile, across the ocean, Sebastian didn't understand what had hit him.

He read the note. Once. Twice.

And then put it away.

He didn't cry. Didn't chase. Didn't talk about her.

Instead, he threw himself into training like a machine. More goals. More press. More headlines.

No distractions. No weaknesses.

From the outside, it looked like he was thriving. Inside, he never asked the real question:

Why didn't I stop her?

Bogotá

Back in Bogotá, Jennifer tried everything: Job applications, consulting projects, Emails to old contacts, but nothing worked. Every rejection chipped away at her sense of direction.

She told her parents she was just "waiting for the right thing." But some nights, she poured a second glass of wine and wondered if she was just waiting for anything at all.

But, everything was silence. At night, the silence rang louder.

Until one day, she got off a bus near the old university.

Just... walking. Her legs took her where her mind never wanted to go. Her old apartment. The one she eventually shared with Felipe.

She stood across the street, under a tree, frozen. And then... the door opened.

There he was. Same confident walk. Same posture. But his face looked different now—softer, calmer.

He was holding a baby. A boy, maybe a year old, just beginning to walk, holding onto his fingers.

And then, the mother stepped out. Young. Natural. Radiant. She had the kind of joy Jennifer hadn't felt in years. Not polished. Not fake. Just... complete.

Felipe kissed the baby's forehead. The mother smiled like the world made sense.

Jennifer didn't cry. She didn't move. She just watched another person living the life she once imagined was hers.

The baby laughed.

And for the first time in a long time, Jennifer felt completely and utterly replaceable.

Jenn went back home and called Katherine Rojas, her college roommate and her lifeline. Kathe was dating a Catalan guy, Pep Cubarsi, who talked too fast and wanted her to move to Barcelona.

Two bottles of wine in, sitting on the kitchen floor.

"I don't know," Kathe said. "What if I hate it?"

"Then we both hate it," Jennifer replied, sipping her wine. "Apply to a PhD with me. Pompeu Fabra. Let's go."

"You're drunk."

"Exactly."

They applied. Both. To the PhD in Economics.

A month later, the emails came.

Jennifer—accepted. Full scholarship. Living stipend. Funding for three years.

Kathe—rejected. But Pompeu offered her a place in the master's instead.

They talked all night.

"Go without me," Kathe said.

"No," Jennifer said firmly. "We go together."

Jennifer didn't tell anyone else. She didn't post anything, explain, or talk about Sebastian. She didn't check if he was still scoring goals. She didn't unblock a single account. She deleted every old match recording. She cleared out the folders with his name. And when her father invited her to go to the stadium, she shook her head.

"No más fútbol, Pa."

That's all she said. And he didn't ask again.

When they boarded the flight to Barcelona, Jennifer looked out the window, her hair tied back, her eyes sharper. She was no longer running. She was rebuilding. And no one—not even she—knew who she would become on the other side.

CHAPTER TWENTY-TWO – BARCELONA DOESN'T HURT

Barcelona didn't feel like home.

But for the first time in a long time... it didn't feel like a wound either.

Jennifer arrived with the basics: one suitcase, a full scholarship, and a heart on airplane mode.

She and Katherine moved into a tiny shared flat in Poblenou, near campus. It had high windows, white walls, and a tired kitchen with a soul of its own. They didn't have much, but every night came with warm food, laughter, and something bubbling in the oven—even if it was just garlic toast and cheap wine.

The first weeks were quiet.

Jennifer barely spoke. She didn't sleep well and dreamed of trains leaving without her, with empty stadiums, or letters without return addresses.

But the academic rhythm pulled her out of herself.

Universitat Pompeu Fabra was fast, demanding, and brilliant.

Her classmates came from India, Italy, Nigeria, and Peru. The seminars were brutal, the debates fiery, the ideas endless.

And finally, she wasn't "his wife."

She was Jennifer.

PhD student.

Economist.

Colombian.

Bilingual.

Sharp.

She was retaking shape.

In her second week, a professor asked her:

"Are you here to write something that changes the world or prove you survived it?"

She didn't hesitate.

"Both."

Katherine began dating again; she was extremely successful with guys in Barcelona.

A Norwegian designer who made her laugh. A Uruguayan who cooked gnocchi with lemon sauce. Jennifer didn't feel jealous.

She felt relieved. Kathe was shining again.

They didn't talk much about London. Some pain only cures with distance.

Jennifer didn't talk about Sebastian. Not to Kathe. Not to anyone.

Sometimes he crept in when she showered, or right before sleep, with his laugh. The way he fell asleep on planes. How alone he must have felt when he woke up and she was gone. But she didn't open the wound. She didn't touch it. She let it stay closed—like a door to a dark room she no longer needed to enter.

On weekends, she walked through El Born, sat in cafés full of noise and strangers, and read books she never finished in Bogotá. Sometimes she took the metro out to quieter beaches, off-season and half-abandoned.

Barcelona had its own rhythm. And unlike London, Bogotá, or Santa Ana—

Barcelona didn't hurt.

After her first draft proposal presentation for the PhD committee, a classmate, Matteo, from Milan, told her:

"Your Spanish sounds like music. And your brain sounds like a war strategist."

She smiled.

"That's the nicest thing anyone's said to me in years."

And for the first time, she didn't feel like he was talking to a version of her shattered by someone else.

He was speaking to her. Only her. But he has no chance.

That night, Jennifer opened her journal. She hadn't written in months. She wrote just one line:

"Maybe I don't need someone to rescue me. Maybe I just needed to see I'm still here."

CHAPTER TWENTY-THREE – EL CLÁSICO

Two years… It had been two whole years since Jennifer had spoken, seen, or heard anything about Sebastian Müller.

Not a photo. Not a scoreline. Not a whisper.

She had buried that world with expert precision.

Barcelona had helped. It didn't care much for Madrid.

And she had been too immersed in data, research, and rebuilding herself to pay attention to transfer windows or LaLiga gossip.

So when Kathe came bouncing into the apartment one Friday afternoon, saying,

"Mikel got us VIP passes to El Clásico this Sunday!",

Jennifer barely reacted. Kathe spun like a teenager.

"He's a partner at Barça. Box seats, free food, the whole thing!"

Jennifer raised an eyebrow. "Isn't this like… religious war level?"

"Exactly. You can't live here and never go to one. This is history."

"I have two deadlines."

"You have two eyes. Use them at the stadium."

Jennifer groaned.

But said yes.

What could possibly go wrong?

The day of the match, Camp Nou roared like a beast.

Jennifer wore a neutral beige coat and had her hair up, which she released during the game. She didn't know any players, and she didn't care. She was there for Kathe and the popcorn (she missed *La Lechona* from El Campin).

They laughed. Took pictures. Cheered politely when Barça scored.

Sebastian Müller never crossed her mind because she didn't know...

She didn't know he'd become one of Real Madrid's star signings over the past summer.

She didn't know his face had been on billboards from Tokyo to Berlin.

She didn't know the world had already called him "Müller II – the architect."

She just... didn't know...

He wasn't in the starting eleven.

Still recovering from a minor knock, he sat with the bench—joggers, hoodie, cap pulled low, sunglasses hiding half his face.

But in minute 43, the coach looked over.

"Warm up."

"Second half?"

The coach nodded. "We need vertical play. You're in."

Sebastian stood up, tied his boots, and jogged toward the pitch edge.

At halftime, the crowd swelled as the bench players began their routine.

He did side steps, high knees, and light touches.

Focused.

Until he heard laughter. Real, belly-deep laughter. From the kiss cam...The stadium camera zoomed in on two people kissing in the VIP zone...

Mikel and Katherine... The crowd whistled. Cheered. Applauded....

Sebastian grinned for half a second... Then froze.

Because next to them... with a laugh that could split the sky— Jennifer.

Even pixelated, even blurry, even though the chaos of the match...

His stomach knotted. The ball rolled past him. He didn't

notice.

His trainer called him. But he couldn't look away from the screen.

Her smile…. Her smile.

The next thing he knew, he was storming toward the sideline.

"Coach!" he barked.

"I'm not going in."

"What?"

"I can't. I'm—something's off."

"You've trained for three weeks—"

"Not today. I'll cost you the game."

The coach cursed under his breath, then signaled to another player. Sebastian threw off his bib, barely thinking, eyes scanning the stands.

He didn't see the kiss cam again. Didn't see the replay. Didn't see anything but her.

When the second half started, he slipped away from the dugout. Security tried to stop him.

He didn't care. He pushed into the hallway.

He went up the stairs, toward the VIP sections.

Jennifer, meanwhile, was sipping wine and talking about Catalan fiscal autonomy with a visiting academic she met in the box. She didn't look toward the pitch. She never saw who didn't come in. She never saw who was looking for her.

The VIP gate was closed when Sebastian reached the top level. Security didn't let him through. He scanned the crowd again, desperate, wild-eyed, and sweating through his hoodie.

She was gone. Or hidden… or just… out of sight.

The match ended 2–2. He never saw the final goal.

That night, Madrid's coach gave a diplomatic excuse to the press:

"He wasn't 100%. No need to risk injury."

But Sebastian didn't sleep. He sat in his hotel room, phone in hand.

Typing her name. Then deleting it. Then typing again. And staring at the screen like it owed him a second chance.

CHAPTER TWENTY-FOUR – DESAPARECIDA

Sebastian couldn't sleep.

The night after El Clásico, he lay on his hotel bed, staring at the ceiling, adrenaline still surging, heart still pounding—not from the match, but from her.

Jennifer… She had been right there.

Next to the kiss cam. Next to that laugh. Next to the life he once held in his hands.

And now?

Now she was gone again.

He reached for his phone. Opened Instagram.

Nothing.

She had deleted her old account ages ago.

He tried Facebook. Searched: Jennifer González.

Thousands.

More if he added "Colombia". Hundreds with similar photos. Tens with photos from old protests, graduation days, filtered sunsets.

He squinted at every image. Heart lurching at every face that almost looked like her.

But none of them were her. He Googled her name.

Every variation he could think of:

Jennifer González

Jennifer Alexandra

Jen González

Yenn González
Ale González

Different spellings, J or Y, one or two N, one or two F. Multiple combinations.

The results led to dead ends—mostly articles from Colombia's past, mentions in student conferences, old research mentions, and blurry posts from NGO blogs.

He clicked through anyway. Each click felt like he was opening a door to a room that no longer had her in it. He found nothing about Barcelona.

Nothing new. No LinkedIn. No conference listings. No academic papers since London.

It was like she had dissolved. Or worse—

Like she had hidden from him on purpose.

He sat on the edge of his bed and muttered, "She blocked me."

He closed his eyes. Pain twisted in his gut.

Just the awful recognition that maybe... she never wanted to be found.

But then he made a mistake. He searched Jennifer González Bogotá again and went too deep into Reddit threads, personal blogs, and archives.

He found an old Colombian article from her university days. It included a photo of her smiling, arms crossed, and wearing a sash that said, "*Graduada con Honores.*" His stomach turned. He had forgotten that version of her—the proud one.

Not the one that left. Not the one he drove away by silence and selfishness.

Still no Barcelona. Still, there was no sign she was anything more than a tourist who passed through his stadium by chance. Maybe it was fate. Perhaps it was God.

The next match was three days later. A home game in Madrid. Packed stadium. High stakes. He started that match. He scored in the 67th minute—beautifully, clinically, like always.

But this time, he didn't run to the crowd.

He pulled off his #27 jersey, revealing a white undershirt. Black letters scrawled in marker:

"WHERE ARE YOU, J?"

The crowd roared, the cameras zoomed in, commentators speculated, Twitter (now X) exploded, and fans guessed it was about a secret girlfriend.

But she didn't respond because she didn't see it. Because she wasn't watching. Because she had stopped watching long ago.

Back in Barcelona, Jennifer was in the library, headphones in, finishing her research outline. She didn't hear the chants and didn't see the post.

Didn't know that the boy she had loved once stood on a world stage, whispering her name to millions...and still couldn't reach her.

CHAPTER TWENTY-FIVE – EL JUEGO DENTRO DEL JUEGO

The goal celebrations started getting strange.

At first, it was just the shirt with "WHERE ARE YOU, J?"

Then the hands were shaped like a "J" over his heart.

Then, the finger went to the sky, traced in the air like cursive. J.A.G.L.

Fans went wild. TikTok exploded. Podcasts launched full theories.

"Is he dating someone secretly?"

"Is it about his mother?"

"Is this part of a brand campaign?"

No one guessed the truth.

No one guessed she was the ghost behind every minute he played.

Sebastian became distracted.

Erratic.

Still brilliant—but heavy. As if he was always trying to find something between the lines of the field.

He watched the kiss cam at every match now. Eyes scanning the crowd obsessively. Looking for the same scarf. The same laugh.

But she never came back. He started ignoring interviews, letting his phone ring, missing brand meetings, and arguing with his agent.

He began checking academic websites late at night, staring at

PhD program listings like they were treasure maps.

One night, he leaned over to Marta, one of his personal assistants—the only one he still trusted.

"I need a favor," he said.

"Anything."

"I want to find a PhD in economics. Somewhere far. Somewhere quiet. Somewhere with a team I can still play for."

She blinked. "Are you serious?"

He nodded.

"I want out of the spotlight. I want real people. I want something... true."

He didn't say her name, but Marta saw it in his eyes. Two weeks later, she returned with a folder.

"Best I could find," she whispered.

Vanderbilt University – Nashville, Tennessee.
Rising program in policy and data. Private. Underrated. Discrete. And with a growing second-division football club aligned to the school's athletic department.

Sebastian took the folder, stared at it, and touched the cover like it was something sacred.

He imagined himself wearing a hoodie, sitting in a seminar room, reading journals, walking across campus in silence, and starting again. And maybe... just maybe...Finding her there.

It wasn't logical, practical, or even clear that she was in the U.S., but he no longer cared.

This wasn't about the Ballon d'Or, or the Bernabéu, or the millions. This was about her and the version of him that only she ever saw. He looked at the crest of Vanderbilt's football club on the last page. A wolf running through trees whispered to itself: "I could disappear here." And maybe... maybe be found.

CHAPTER TWENTY-SIX – SOMBRAS PARALELAS

Jennifer hadn't thought about Sebastian in weeks. Not really. Not with emotion, not with longing, not even with regret. But Felipe... Felipe had been everywhere lately.

In her vocabulary. In her phrasing. In the way she corrected her students. In the way she judged herself after speaking too long in a seminar. She was becoming him. And she couldn't tell if that made her proud or... terrified.

She kept seeing his shadow in the corners of the classrooms. In baby strollers across the street.

In the way someone ordered their espresso, in every sharp, or any articulate man in a navy jacket who interrupted someone with confidence. She kept hearing his voice in her own.

Was this growth? Or repetition?

She had left Felipe years ago and then left Sebastian without a trace. Now she stood alone, watching herself evolve into something she couldn't recognize.

Was this her version of success?

Or was it just the version he wanted for her?

Her anxiety didn't come in screams. It came in spirals. Late at night.

Under fluorescent lights.

In conversations she had with herself, but never said aloud.

And it reached a peak the night she was accepted to present her Job Market Paper at a top European conference.

She told herself it was fine, professional, and safe in Madrid until she read the keynote list.

Felipe Santos.

University of Chicago.

Global leader in trade policy and political economy.

One of the youngest professors ever tenured.

And, apparently, still magnetic as hell. She almost pulled out of the conference. Almost, but Katherine talked her down.

"You said you were writing your own story," Kathe said over wine. "You don't write it by skipping chapters."

So, Jennifer went. Nervous, Prepared. Dignified. And her paper... shone

It was the final session before lunch. A small room, a packed audience. The applause was genuine, the questions sharp, and the award at the end? Unexpected.

Best Job Market Presentation.

She stood there, stunned, as strangers shook her hand and whispered, "Brilliant" and "You have a future here." But none of that made her hands sweat like the sight of him in the back row.

Felipe. Cool. Still. Proud. Watching.

She walked past him without speaking after the session, but her heart didn't settle. She couldn't sleep. The next morning, before the final panel, she found him outside, sipping café alone under a tree. She stood there for a full minute before speaking.

"Didn't think you'd stay for my session."

He looked up, surprised. Then smiled softly.

"You always underestimate how proud I am of you."

Her stomach turned. Silence stretched between them like a tightrope. He gestured to the chair across from him.

"Coffee tomorrow? Just us. No ghosts. No past."

She hesitated. Then nodded. And walked away without saying anything else.

That night, in her hotel room, she stared at the ceiling. Not because of Sebastian. Not because of Felipe. Because she couldn't tell who she was becoming anymore, which scared her more than either of them ever had.

CHAPTER TWENTY-SEVEN – EL ÚLTIMO GOLPE DE LA ESTRELLA

The press said Sebastian Müller was at his peak.

"Unstoppable."

"Müller II is no longer a promise—he's now."

"Ballon d'Or contender."

But Sebastian only felt noise, Matches, Headlines, Flashbulbs, and at night... emptiness. Loneliness.

After the shirt message — WHERE ARE YOU, J? — he waited. No messages. No unknown calls.

No mysterious crowd appearances. Nothing. It was as if the world had swallowed her whole. Or even worse, as if it was protecting her from him. And slowly, quietly, he started to accept it. Not from resignation, from change.

"What would you do if you could start over?" Marta, his assistant, asked one night after training.

He didn't hesitate.

"I'd never touch a ball."

"I'd study. Walk to class. Be invisible."

She laughed. "You're famous on four continents, Bastian."

"Then I need a fifth."

The Vanderbilt University folder wasn't in his drawer anymore. It was everywhere: In his gym bag, bed, and thoughts.

Late at night, he read the course list like scripture:

* Quantitative Methods.
* Political Economy.
* Behavioral Game Theory.
* Applied Ethics in Public Policy.

It didn't sound like escape, it sounded like oxygen.

He asked his lawyer for full confidentiality. He told Marta, "Prepare the application. No one should know it's me."

She raised an eyebrow. "What about the club?"

He shook his head. "Not yet." To the press, he offered excuses: Fatigue, squad rotation, personal recovery time, but inside, he was already there.

In Nashville. Wearing a hoodie, holding a coffee, and being no one. And, just maybe, becoming the man she once saw in him, long before the world crowned him.

One night, Marta brought in the final draft of the PhD application.

He stared at the screen. His name was at the bottom. His answers were honest. There was no image management or media team—just him. He clicked "Submit" and closed the laptop.

In the next Champions League match, he scored a beauty—he cut through three defenders and curled it into the top corner. The stadium exploded. But he didn't run, he didn't raise his arms, nor point to the sky. He dropped to one knee, stared at the ground, and said nothing.

The media called it "spiritual"; for him, it was a goodbye.

CHAPTER TWENTY-EIGHT – THE COFFEE THAT WASN'T JUST COFFEE

Jennifer had changed outfits three times. She did not like any of them because they were too serious, casual, or intentional. She settled on something in the middle: jeans, blazer, soft lipstick, hair half up. She told herself it wasn't a date. It was just coffee. But her heart said otherwise, and so did the quiet panic in her chest.

She wasn't going to bring up the baby. She wasn't going to mention the woman in Bogotá. She wouldn't admit how many nights that image had haunted her—the life that wasn't hers being lived by someone else. But those questions were burning at the top of her mind; they were boiling on her lips. Was he married? Was that child his? Had she been replaced… completely? She didn't know what she wanted to hear; she only needed to hear something.

When she arrived, Felipe was already there. He was wearing a dark sweater with rolled sleeves, and his neatly trimmed hair. He had the same scent and the same calm. He stood up and opened his arms without hesitation.

She froze, just for a second.

Then stepped in.

The hug was warm. Familiar. Maybe, too much. For a moment, her body forgot how to keep its distance. Because for years, this had been the only place where her anxiety stopped screaming.

When she pulled away, she tried to play it cool. He didn't. He looked straight at her and said, without prelude:

"I love you."

Jennifer blinked. Everything in her tilted sideways.

"What?" she whispered.

Felipe didn't move.

"I love you."

And then, like nothing had happened, he turned and walked to the counter to get the coffees they had ordered ahead.

She sat there, frozen. No script. No emotional shield. No sarcasm. No plan. Just a pounding in her chest and the feeling that she had just jumped timelines.

When he returned, he gently set the cup down in front of her. She looked up and smiled, just like before: before London, Sebastian, or the loss. She let the moment take her.

He didn't repeat the phrase again. Not out loud. But it sat between them like a third person at the table.

She sipped her coffee. Cleared her throat.

"Was that your baby?" she asked softly, telling herself she should not have done that.

He tilted his head. Smiled.

"No. That's David—my nephew."

"And the woman?" she replied, lifting her left eyebrow.

"My sister-in-law. They've been staying in my old apartment since I left for Chicago. It's close to her work."

Jennifer let out a breath she didn't realize she was holding. She looked down at her cup, trying to hide it. But he saw it anyway and didn't say a word.

She wasn't sure what that relief meant, or why it mattered, but she couldn't deny it: something opened up inside her again. Possibility, memory. Maybe even... curiosity.

Felipe reached for a sugar packet, distracted, and Jennifer, staring into her coffee, whispered just loud enough for the table to hear:

"You really meant it." -about his particular way to say "hello"
that day-
    He didn't look up.
    "Always have."

CHAPTER TWENTY-NINE – WHAT NEVER LEFT

Something had cracked wide open.

Since the coffee with Felipe, Jennifer had tried to distract herself—papers, lectures, dinners with Kathe, long walks by the beach, but nothing could silence the echo of those words.

"I love you."

Not shouted or begged. Those words were just placed on the table like a fact, and that's what made it dangerous.

But the real problem came with the "Always have", because it felt real. Not poetic, romanticized, or rehearsed, just... true.

What she felt now wasn't like before. It wasn't adrenaline or butterflies. It wasn't teenage chaos. Now, it was clarity, deeper, unshakable. And, it terrified her.

By the third sleepless night, Jennifer couldn't take it anymore. She stared at her phone screen for ten minutes, her thumb hovered. She didn't want him to answer, but she didn't want to leave it unsaid. She called... One ring. Two.

"Jenn?"

His voice was soft. Gentle. Still his.

"Hi."

"Didn't expect to hear from you so soon."

"I didn't expect to call."

He waited.

She didn't hold back.

"You don't love me."

"You didn't look for me."

"You didn't come the day I graduated."

Silence... Long. Heavy. Then he said, calmly:

"Do you want to hear what you want to hear or the truth?"

She swallowed.

"Tell me the truth."

His voice didn't waver.

"I've always loved you. I still do."

"I didn't show up because I wanted to see you win on your own."

"Because I was proud to see you shine, not because I was there——but because you were."

She was quiet. Her breathing shallow. Then she asked, almost in a whisper:

"Have you been watching me?"

"Always."

And then, the question she hadn't dared ask since Bogotá:

"Did you see me with Sebastian?"

Another pause. Then:

"Yes."

The air went out of her lungs. She closed her eyes.

"And you didn't do anything?"

Her voice cracked.

"You didn't feel anything?"

His answer came softly:

"I felt everything."

"But I learned how to live without you."

"Not how to stop loving you."

Jennifer bit her lip. Everything inside her was shaking. And he wasn't even trying to shake her. That's what made her angry.

"Why didn't you fight for me?"

He answered without flinching.

"Because love isn't a war."

"It's not always impulse or possession."

"It's letting you be happy, even if that means without me."

Silence again.

Then he added:

"Love that only exists when it's convenient isn't love, Jennifer."

"And I never stopped feeling it."

She didn't know what to say. Because no one had ever loved her like that. Not Sebastian.

Not even herself.

CHAPTER THIRTY –
THE INVISIBLE LEAP

Sebastian Müller landed in Nashville on a cloudy Tuesday afternoon. There was no press, screaming fans, contract announcements, no gold-embroidered jerseys. There was just a backpack, a university-issued hoodie, and silence.

He had finally become invisible. And for the first time in years... it felt good.

The plan was simple: two years of full-time study, then, if all went well, a jump to the MLS with Nashville SC in year three—already pre-negotiated, quietly, no fanfare.

But first: exams, econometrics, public policy seminars, long nights in libraries, and the campus football league. That was the deal. No headlines or sponsor obligations. Just... student life.

The rumors had leaked anyway. A TA in the admissions office told someone on the Econ Football Team. By the time he got to the dorm, the hallway was full of whispers:

"It's him." "No way." "Dude, our team's gonna win something this year."

They had assigned him the biggest room in the dorm—technically reserved for visiting fellows, but no one argued. It had a mini fridge, a desk with two monitors, and a whiteboard already half-filled with supply-demand diagrams someone had drawn in excitement.

On the bed was a folder: "Welcome to Vanderbilt." And two Jerseys: #10 and #27; they want him to choose.

Inside the folder, his syllabus, a campus map, a campus football league schedule...

...and a note written in messy handwriting:

"You're our only shot at not finishing last this year. No pressure.

– Econ FC"

He laughed. For the first time in months.

The next morning, he showed up at the first practice. There were no cleats, no locker room, just a field, two torn nets, and fifteen students with varying degrees of cardio.

The coach?

A second-year student from Nigeria named Tochukwu, PhD candidate in environmental economics.

"Sebas," he said with a grin, "if you score at least once per game, you don't even have to defend." Sebastian shook his head. "Fair."

In his first match, he wore the plain blue team shirt with the number 10 scribbled on the back in permanent marker. The sidelines were full of econ nerds eating granola and holding handmade signs.

He scored just six goals and switched to goalie. The Econ program beated the current champions, the Law faculty, 6–2.

Someone started chanting things, and he had no idea what they meant, but he chanted too.

At night, alone in his dorm, Sebastian sat at his desk and opened his laptop.

He wasn't looking for highlights, or interviews, or news. He opened his reading for Development Economics. And for once... He wasn't running from anything. He was building something, and maybe—just maybe— waiting for someone to find him here.

CHAPTER THIRTY-ONE – THE MAN STARTING OVER

Days in Nashville began to blur. Mornings meant lectures on microeconomic Theory, Econometrics, Policy, and ethics. Afternoons were filled with group projects, reading, and football practice. The evenings were quiet: books, stretching, and sometimes a walk under the oak trees near the river trail.

His classmates didn't treat him like a star. At first, they were hesitant, curious, polite, and unsure if the rumors were real. But once he answered a problem set question with a confused *"¿qué es esto?"* in a perfect European Spanish accent, he was adopted.

"You're one of us now," someone said.

He was no longer the Müller. He was Sebas. A tall German-Colombian-Gringo with a football addiction and a newly discovered love for labor economics.

He wasn't the best student, but he tried. He asked questions, stayed late in the TA sessions, rewrote his notes after class, and googled words he didn't understand, leaving sticky notes all over his books. When he didn't understand something, he muttered to himself: "She would explain it better..." And then he kept going.

On campus, he kept a low profile. He wore hoodies. Tucked his curls under a cap. Ate in the dining hall like anyone else.

And yet... people started to notice him again, not because of his goals, but because of how present he was. He listened. He helped classmates revise presentations. He started a WhatsApp group for study notes and Econ FC memes. When he scored on the field, he didn't celebrate—he simply smiled.

One Saturday, after a hard-fought 2–1 win over the Business School, he stayed back to collect the cones. Tochukwu came up behind him.

"Hey," he said. "You okay?"

Sebastian looked up.

"I think I'm starting to like who I am here."

Tochukwu nodded. "You were always this guy. You just forgot."

That night, Sebastian opened his old private photo folder- the one he hadn't dared to open in years. There she was: Jennifer, sleeping with a textbook on her chest, Jennifer, laughing with the twins, Jennifer, holding his hand after his first injury.

He didn't cry. He didn't try to delete the pictures. He just looked at her and whispered:

"I hope you're becoming who you always wanted to be." And for the first time in a long, long time— He meant it without pain.

CHAPTER THIRTY-TWO – PARIS WAS HIM

Jennifer didn't know how she had ended up back in this place. Sending "muahs". Staring at her phone screen at odd hours. Second-guessing whether it was too early or too late to send a "What are you thinking about?" But there she was. Again. Older. Wiser. Calmer. Yet still entirely his when it came to Felipe. Since that coffee in Madrid, they hadn't stopped messaging.

At first, once a day. Then twice. Then... she'd catch herself unlocking her phone just to see if he had responded. And he always did. Sometimes quickly. Sometimes after hours. But always.

There was something in the way he wrote that brought her back to herself. Every time.

One quiet afternoon, while eating lunch alone in a café in El Born, she typed:

"Where are you today?"

He answered thirty minutes later:

"Paris. Visiting professor for the next few months."

She stopped mid-bite.

Paris... Within minutes, she had three tabs open—flights, train tickets, and hotels. She didn't know if it was impulsive. But she did know one thing: She hadn't felt this way since that kiss in the airport with Sebastian.

After days of increasingly charged messages, she broke the tension.

"If I show up, will you be there?"

His reply came, soft as ever:

"I never left."

She arrived Friday afternoon, wearing a light coat and dark sunglasses. Her lips were dry from nerves. Paris didn't feel like the movies; it felt real because he was there.

When she saw him waiting outside the metro station—tall, calm, unshaken— she didn't wait. She walked straight to him, touched his chest, looked into his eyes, and said:

"I love you."

He didn't smile or blink. He replied, "Explain it to me." She froze.

Because he always did that. Broke her with the truth. And she just laughed softly while she wanted to slap him, laugh, and scream.

"Damn you," she whispered.

He stepped forward and held her like nothing had changed.

The weekend passed like a dream she already knew by heart —but this time didn't want to wake from. They made love as if they had never stopped, as though years, heartbreak, and oceans had merely been a brief intermission.

It wasn't just good; it was safe, clear, and certain.

And as she lay on his chest, tangled, warm, and still breathless, she asked herself: "What was I doing away from this for so long?"

On Sunday afternoon, with the windows open and Paris buzzing with footsteps, bells, and a gentle breeze, Jennifer checked her phone. 33 missed calls. Kathe. Texts.

"Where the hell are you?"

"Jenn?? Are you alive??"

"You disappeared since FRIDAY."

Jennifer smiled, exhaled, and looked over at Felipe, who was reading an article with his glasses sliding down his nose. Paris was beautiful, but he made it home.

CHAPTER THIRTY-THREE – GRAVITY

The flight back to Barcelona felt longer than it should have. Jennifer stared out the window for most of the way. Silent. Still. Paris had been... What? A reset? A mistake? A homecoming? She didn't know. But she knew this: she hadn't felt that alive, that wanted, that understood in years. Not since Bogotá. Not since that classroom. Not since before she became someone else's shadow.

Kathe was waiting when she arrived at the apartment, her hair in a bun, socks mismatched, and arms crossed. "You look like someone who just came back from a cult," she said flatly.

Jennifer set her bag down. "I'm fine."

"Thirty-three missed calls, Jenn."

"I know."

"Three days. Not even a text."

"I know."

Kathe stared at her. "Was it him?"

Jennifer nodded.

Kathe didn't speak. She just went to the kitchen and poured two glasses of wine.

They sat on the couch, side by side, not touching. Jennifer finally whispered:

"It felt like the part of me I thought was gone... came back."

Kathe didn't blink. "Do you love him?"

Jennifer exhaled.

"I think I never stopped."

The next morning, the city moved on as if nothing had

happened. Classes. Trams. Tourists. Deadlines. But Jennifer couldn't fall back into rhythm. Felipe texted her before sunrise:

"You feel different now, but you always were."

She didn't answer right away.

Not because she didn't want to, but because for once... she wasn't rushing toward the feeling.
She was trying to understand it.

In class, her professor praised her most recent draft.

"Your work's evolved," he said. "It feels more like a woman who knows what she's trying to say."

Jennifer smiled, because for the first time, she really did.

Still, that night, alone in her room, curled up with a blanket and her laptop open to a blank document... she wondered:

"Is loving him still a chapter of my life... or is it the title?"

And before closing her eyes, she opened her messages and typed one line:

"If you asked me to stay in Paris... I don't think I'd say no." She didn't hit send.

She saved it as a draft. Sometimes, that's how gravity works. It doesn't crash you down; it just pulls.

CHAPTER THIRTY-FOUR – WHERE THE HEART LIVES

Jennifer didn't sleep much that night. She kept waking up, thinking about Paris.

Thinking about the way he looked at her. The way he didn't chase her or beg her. He just opened the door and let her walk in.

She checked her phone thrice and read her typed message: "If you asked me to stay in Paris… I don't think I'd say no." She kept it as a draft, but the moment her alarm rang and the sky was still purple with morning, she hit send.

Just like that. No edits. No filter. Just truth.

Felipe's reply came two hours later. She hadn't even heard the notification. She was brushing her teeth when her screen lit up. One line.

"My home is your home, Jenn."

And then, right below it:

"You can stay. You can leave. You can return. That's the point of home."

"But heart… that's something else."

Her hand froze mid-air, toothbrush still in her mouth. She reread it.

"Home is not always the same as heart."

She sat down on the edge of her bed, still holding the phone, her breath shallow. She understood. He was offering her freedom.

Not a life in Paris. Not a plan. Not a ring or a label.

But a place where she could exist fully, messily, and still be welcomed.

And yet... he was also drawing a quiet boundary. She could stay, but she had to choose the heart too. Not just the geography.

All morning, she couldn't stop thinking about it. Not in class, not over coffee, and not even when Kathe tried to gossip about Pep's latest romantic fail. Jennifer's heart was somewhere else, and for once, it wasn't confused.

That night, she replied. I've had many homes. But you were the first person who ever felt like one. I want both: home and heart. But I'm scared that if I come, I'll forget how to leave again. The message was marked read within minutes.

But there was no reply. Not yet.

Just three dots pulsing on the screen... then gone.

She put the phone down, climbed into bed, and stared at the ceiling. If this was love, it wasn't the kind that asked her to lose herself; it was the kind that dared her to find herself inside someone else. For the first time, that didn't feel like weakness. It felt like peace.

CHAPTER THIRTY-FIVE – TRYING WITH BOTH HANDS

Jennifer couldn't sit still. The message hadn't left her mind. Felipe's response — "My home is your home... but heart is something else." It wasn't rejection. It was an invitation. But only if she walked in fully. And she was tired of half-doors.

So she texted again. It was not long, it was not poetic, it was just the truth, plain and clear:

"I want to try. Really try. All in, but not alone. I want to grow with you — learn, make mistakes, love freely. But I can't feel like I depend on you to exist. I need to feel safe, not trapped.
Can we build something where I'm still... me?"

She stared at the screen after hitting send. This time, there was no backup message, emoji, or " muah." Just the core.

His answer came twenty minutes later. As always, effortlessly him:

"I never wanted a version of you that needed me. I want the version that chooses me. We'll build it slowly. Free. Honest. We'll learn each other again, but no one leaves without saying goodbye this time."

Then a second message.

"Let's begin again, Jenn. No pressure. Just you and me, choosing each other. One day at a time."

She burst into tears. Not because it hurt, but because it didn't. Because it felt safe. It felt possible. It felt mutual.

That night, she called him.

No text. No video. Just voice.

He picked up with a *"Hola."*

She smiled into the receiver.

"I think this time... we'll get it right."

He chuckled. "This time, we know what we're risking, and what we're worth."

A new rhythm began.

Daily calls. Random voice notes. Silly memes about economic models. Flirty messages that turned into full confessions. Conversations about politics, poetry, and pain. They didn't rush. They didn't label it. But it was them. And that was enough. For now.

Jennifer felt the difference. This wasn't romance meant to save her. It was romance that acknowledged her. For the first time in years, her heart didn't feel like it was trying to win something; it felt like it had found its place to rest.

CHAPTER THIRTY-SIX – A LOVE YOU GROW INTO

The first few weeks after Paris were strange. Not dramatic. Not uncertain. Just... new.

Jennifer returned to Barcelona with a calm she hadn't felt in years. Not the kind you get from answers, but from choosing something and watching it choose you back.

She and Felipe didn't talk about the future in bold letters.

No "what are we now?"

No "where is this going?"

They just... talked. Every day. Every night. About papers, their students, coffee brands, broken printers, and bad weather.

And every once in a while... about love. Not just as a word, but as a practice.

Jennifer wrote more, laughed more, and worried less. She was still herself, but more grounded and less haunted. Being with Felipe didn't make her forget the past; it just made it feel lighter.

Fairfax, Virginia. Prosperity Avenue. Uscis Field Office (Today).

"Did you ever tell him about the loss?" The voice interrupted her train of thought.

Jennifer blinked, pulled from the story. Back to the present.

To the interview room in Fairfax, Virginia.

To the USCIS officer flipping through paperwork.

The woman was now standing, slightly hesitating before heading toward the restroom.

Jennifer sat up straighter. "No," she said softly. "Not then. Not in Paris."

The officer looked back. "Not even when you went to see him?"

Jennifer shook her head.

"That conversation didn't come until... my second divorce with Sebastian."

A long pause. Then the woman nodded. "Alright. I'll be right back."

And she stepped out, heels clicking down the hallway.

Jennifer looked down at her hands. Funny how a life could be made of erasures: of when things were said and when they weren't. The miscarriage. The silence. The second divorce.

She had lived whole lifetimes between the versions of herself that were brave enough to speak.

Back in Paris that spring, she hadn't spoken about the loss, or Sebastian, or Bogotá. But she had felt safe again, and sometimes, that was the only conversation her heart was ready for.

One night, Felipe called her just to say:

"I can't wait to love you without memory. Just now."

And she answered:

"Then let's begin again. Without comparison. Without ghosts."

They were no longer trying to reclaim what they once had; they were building something new.

A love they had grown into.

Not because of time, but because of everything it had taken to get there.

CHAPTER THIRTY-SEVEN – THE DECADE THAT WAS ALWAYS OURS

Jennifer turned thirty on a Wednesday, on a sunny yet windy day in fall. No party. No drama. Just Felipe, a small dinner in Montmartre, and a cake with too much chocolate. He had told her, weeks before:

"I want this year to be soft for you. Like a secret."

And somehow, he meant it. No pressure. No plans. Just mornings filled with books, nights filled with voice notes, and weekends where they were simply Jenn and Felipe again.

But a date was coming. One she hadn't dared to say out loud before. Ten years. Not ten years together. Not even ten years as a couple. But ten years of having each other in some form.

In silence. In memory. In letters never sent. In airport thoughts. In whispered names during other people's dreams.

"I don't want to let it pass," she told him over breakfast one morning.

Felipe looked up from his laptop. "Pass what?"

"The decade," she said.

His eyes softened. He reached for her hand.

"Then let's celebrate it."

They planned nothing extravagant—just a weekend trip somewhere quiet, with wine, jazz, and maybe a rooftop—just the two of them.

Jennifer felt it in her chest — something she hadn't known for years.

Certainty.

Not perfection. Not fantasy. Just that they had finally found the same beat if love had a rhythm.

The days leading up to the trip were full of warm calls, playful teasing, and emails titled:

"Decade Itinerary, Version 4, With the Good Cheese."

Felipe booked the hotel, Jennifer picked the music, printed photos, and bought a red dress that made her feel dangerous and soft all at once.

On the night before the trip, Felipe sent her a message that made her cry softly into her pillow:

"You've always been my longest chapter, and maybe... we're finally ready to write the ending together."

She replied:

"Not an ending. Let's start part two."

They were leaving early the next morning. She had her suitcase ready, with shoes by the door, a music playlist already downloaded, and her passport in her purse. And her heart? Finally, whole again.

CHAPTER THIRTY-EIGHT – NOT THAT STAGE ANYMORE

Sebastian had begun to smile again. Not the smile for cameras. Not the performance smile.

But quiet ones — while solving equations, or scoring in the Econ FC intramural league, or sharing bad takeout with his classmates after midnight debates about tax policy. He was slowly becoming someone else.

Not entirely new. Just... lighter. Less haunted.

He'd even gone on a few dates. Casual ones. A literature student from Chile. A barista who studied urban planning. A musician who didn't care about football but said he had a "Nobel face." They were fine; nothing that impressed him. However, he was kind, yet he remained distant. None of them were her, but they didn't need to be. He wasn't chasing anymore; he was focusing. On now. On who he was becoming.

Until that concert, he almost didn't go — invited last-minute by one of his econ teammates whose sister worked in PR. It was a popular R&B singer, famous in the U.S., less so globally. Sebastian didn't recognize her name and didn't care. He just wanted music and lights for one night. He wore a cap, kept his head down, and stayed in the back.

Halfway through the show, during the interlude, the lights shifted toward the crowd. She spoke, voice velvet-smooth: "We got someone special in the room tonight."

He froze.

She looked directly where he was standing.

"I've never seen you off the field, Müller. You clean up real good."

The crowd roared. Phones were out. He blinked. And cursed under his breath.

Ten minutes later, backstage security found him.

"She'd love to meet you," the man said.

Sebastian wanted to say no. But didn't. Maybe curiosity. Maybe pressure. He followed.

She was beautiful. Sharp. Flirty. The kind of presence that sucked air from the room.

They talked. He barely spoke.

She thought she was in control. She touched his hand, then held it while talking to him to come to the stage. He did not know how to stop it, or if he wanted to. Somehow, it was a quick return to the center of the stage. The lights, the music, her voice, her eyes captivated him, enchanting him to the middle of the stage, just where all the spotlights pointed. The crowd roared, and just at that moment, she kissed him. Hard. It felt like an ice bucket on his head. There were flashes — somewhere, somehow. He pulled away, wiped his mouth, stepped back, and said:

"I'm not that stage anymore."

She tilted her head, confused. "Excuse me?"

He just nodded once and left.

The next day, he deactivated his social media again. He called Marta.

"Start signing me up for conferences."

She hesitated. "Any preference?"

"Yes," he said. "Wherever there's a decent econ department and good coffee."

"But what's the strategy?"

He hesitated. And then said the quiet part out loud:

"I'm fishing."

"For what?"

He looked out the window of the student library, past the oak trees and into nothing.

"For a name I might see on a list."
He didn't say her name.
He didn't have to.

CHAPTER THIRTY-NINE – THE DREAM YOU FORGOT TO WANT

Paris shimmered that weekend. It wasn't the Eiffel Tower, the music, or the wine. It was them. Ten years. Not linear. Not tidy. But theirs. They laughed over old memories, danced barefoot in the hotel room, and took blurry photos in a photo booth they found tucked behind a bookstore. Jennifer hadn't felt this close, this sure, in years.

And with Felipe, that certainty came like breath. Effortless. Quiet.

The hotel room was dim and warm. Jazz played low on a speaker. They were lying in bed, tangled, the air still thick with softness. Her head rested on his chest, his fingers tracing invisible circles on her back. Then he said it.

Softly. Dreamily.

"I've always wanted a family with you."

She froze.

He didn't notice.

"I used to dream about it back then. You, walking around barefoot with tea. A baby crying in the next room."

Jennifer stared at the ceiling, breath locked in her chest.

He went on.

"I think you're the only woman in the world I could have a child with. Like... really want one. Maybe two."

She didn't move.

"Definitely one like you," he said.

"Big eyes. Barefoot. Brilliant. With your laugh that only shows when you're not watching."

He thought he was being romantic. He was.

But her world shattered quietly under the weight of those words.

Felipe didn't know. He had never known. Not about Bogotá. Not about the test. The bathroom. The silent sobbing. The hospital. And certainly not about what was lost.

She had never told him, and she wouldn't now.

She smiled faintly. Kissed his shoulder. Said nothing.

That night, when he fell asleep — chest rising and falling, arms around her — Jennifer lay awake, skin still bare, eyes wide open in the dark. Her hand moved slowly for her phone. She typed quietly.

"Can I get pregnant after a miscarriage?"

"Fertility after loss."

"What if I haven't gotten pregnant again?"

She hadn't been careful with birth control. Not with Bastian. Not since. But nothing had ever happened. The thought spiraled rapidly, twisting in her gut like a storm. The pain. The guilt. The wondering. Was it her body? Was it her mind? Was it punishment?

She curled up tighter under the covers. Felipe murmured something in his sleep. She didn't respond. She didn't move. She just stared at the time on her phone until it turned 3:00 a.m. Then 4:00. Then 5:30.

Her flight to Barcelona was at noon. Her thesis defense was the next day. Graduation was in a week. All things she had dreamed about. But as she packed the next morning, her hands trembled slightly. Felipe kissed her goodbye at the door and told her he'd be there for the ceremony if she wanted.

She smiled and told him she did.

He waved once and closed the door.

On the flight, Jennifer stared out the window the entire

way. Not because the view was beautiful, but because her own reflection wasn't. She didn't recognize the woman in the glass, and for the first time in a long time, she didn't know what kind of future she deserved.

CHAPTER FORTY – THE QUEEN'S GAMBIT

Sebastian had now presented at twelve conferences worldwide: Berlin, Buenos Aires, Geneva, Toronto, Seoul. Every time, the same pattern emerged: Check-in, keynote, nervous students, cheap coffee, and no Jennifer.

He never said her name.

But each name tag he glanced at, each participant list he scrolled through, held the same unspoken hope. She was never there.

Until one conference in Oslo, something shifted.

Her name was Camille. She entered the plenary session with the stillness of someone used to attention. French. Flawless posture. 5'10" of elegance and 121 pounds of effortless body perfection. Sebastian didn't notice her at first. But she noticed him.

After the panel, she approached him with a confidence that wasn't performative — just natural.

"I used to have your poster on my wall," she said, accent crisp, smile enigmatic.

He blinked. "I'm flattered."

"Number 27. Real Madrid. You were the reason I got into football."

He raised an eyebrow. "You played?"

"Left wing," she nodded. "Fast and annoyingly smart."

He laughed. Then she added:

"My brother was on the French team that beat you in the U19 Euro final."

Sebastian smiled widely, the memory punching him with both pride and old pain.

"You just made me feel old and a venged."

She introduced herself fully: "Nice to meet you, Mr. Müller. My name is Camille Moreau. I hold a law degree from Sciences Po and am a PhD candidate in AI technology ethics at MIT, where I research AI policy in developing countries. Additionally, I enjoy playing chess; in fact, I am a Grandmaster, but people tend to know me because I participated in Miss Universe representing France."

He almost choked on his espresso. "Sorry, what?"

She smiled. "It's a long story."

It wasn't love at first sight. It was something subtler, quieter: recognition.

She had run from glitter, too, turning down TV offers, fashion empires, and acting schools. She wanted to be taken seriously, so she studied and kept studying.

They began texting, first about conferences, then chess tournaments, then books, and finally just to say hi.

They started attending events with the hope the other would

be there. He'd send a message:

"Going to Lisbon AI conf?"

She'd reply:

"Only if you let me beat you in blitz chess again."

They met halfway across the world, pretending it was a coincidence.

She once told him, "I didn't expect to find someone else who hated being famous."

And he had replied:

"I didn't expect to find someone who made me forget I ever was."

Camille was more than beautiful. She was dangerous—not with seduction, but with insight. She could dismantle an argument with a single sentence. She played chess like a poet. She listened like a therapist. And her silences made Sebastian think harder than most lectures.

They never defined anything. But there was a tension between them — sharp and warm, like candlelight in a cathedral. And one night in Vienna, after a closing dinner...

She turned to him and said, "We should be careful."

He tilted his head. "Of what?"

She looked at him long and steadily.

"Of becoming too important to each other."

He didn't know how to answer. Because deep down, he already feared she was.

CHAPTER FORTY-ONE – A PERFECT DAY WITH A SHADOW

Barcelona was glowing, with a blue sky, the late spring sun, and olive trees in bloom. It felt as if the city had dressed up just for her. Jennifer stood in front of the mirror in her robe, while her cap and gown were folded neatly on the bed. Her thesis had been defended, and her name was confirmed on the program. She was about to become Doctor Jennifer Alexandra González López. She should have been floating, but something tugged at her ribs like a loose thread.

Felipe was flying that morning. He had promised to be there. He always kept his promises. That wasn't the problem. The issue was something quieter, more internal—something like...

"What happens when you get everything you worked for... but still feel afraid?"

Her makeup was subtle. Her hair was soft and half-down. She chose her favorite lipstick—not too bold, not too quiet. Kathe helped zip her gown.

"You good?" she asked, smiling but watching her closely.

Jennifer nodded. "Perfect." A lie she had practiced well.

The ceremony was beautiful. Applause. Flowers. The words "cum laude" attached to her name.

Felipe arrived just in time, his eyes tired but proud. He kissed her forehead and clapped harder than anyone when her name was called. Mouthed "I love you" when she returned to her seat.

And she smiled back, full, radiant, present. But inside... A flicker.

At the reception, he held her hand tightly that night as people congratulated her. "You made this real," he whispered once. And then later, over wine, casually, tenderly— He said it again:

"You'd be an incredible mother."

She froze for a second too long. He didn't notice. She changed the subject before her throat betrayed her.

Back in the apartment, after everyone had left and the silence wrapped around her like fog—she sat alone on her bed. Dress on the chair. Gown on the floor. Her phone glowing. Felipe had gone back to his hotel. They agreed she needed space to rest, to process. She had insisted. He respected that.

But she couldn't rest. She opened her notes app and typed the same words she hadn't said aloud:

"What if I can't be what he thinks I am?"

"What if I can never carry a child again?"

"What if I never could?"

"What if I've been writing futures for other people and forgot to imagine my own?"

She closed her eyes and felt the weight of joy and grief colliding in her chest.

Graduation day. A perfect day. But there was a shadow in every photo she took. And no one else could see it.

CHAPTER FORTY-TWO – BETWEEN MOVES

Camille didn't rush anything. Not her arguments. Not her chess openings. Not her feelings. This made Sebastian all the more drawn to her. She wasn't fire; she was calculation. Yet her presence was warm, not cold. Precise, but never mechanical.

They saw each other now more often: in conferences, in cafés between panels, and in hotels booked too far apart to be coincidence. Sometimes they shared a bottle of wine and debated ethics.

Other times, they didn't speak at all — just moved chess pieces for hours, letting the silence hold them together.

One night, in Zurich, she beat him in five moves. He looked up, stunned.

"Seriously?"

She raised an eyebrow.

"I gave you the Queen, and you didn't take it," she said, voice low.

"Why?"

He shrugged.

"Maybe I didn't believe it was really mine."

Her expression softened.

"You still play like you're scared of winning."

Sebastian looked down at the board. And didn't answer.

They weren't lovers. Not officially. Not yet. But one night in Lisbon, after a panel on machine learning ethics, they walked through the old town. It was late, quiet, almost cinematic. They stopped at a fountain. She leaned against the wall, and he stood in front of her. And she whispered:

"What are we doing?"

He hesitated. Then, answered honestly:

"I think we're trying not to fall in love while knowing exactly what's happening."

She smiled, said nothing, but reached for his hand and held it like a secret. He never compared her to Jennifer. He couldn't. Camille was a different melody—one that didn't remind him of who he had been but of who he could still become. With her, the weight of being "Müller" faded. She called him Bastian. She listened to his ideas before his highlights. She once said: "You're more interesting now than you ever were on a field." And somehow, it didn't feel like a compliment. It felt like the truth.

One morning, after a quiet breakfast and shared coffee in a Berlin hotel, Camille looked up from her phone and said:

"I want you to meet my parents."

Sebastian blinked. She continued, calm but sincere:

"They're in Nice. My father's a famous lawyer, and my mother's a bureaucrat obsessed with policy reform. They'll love you. Or interrogate you. Possibly both."

He smiled, unsure.

"I didn't think we were—"

"You don't have to be anything official," she interrupted. "But we're not invisible either. And I don't bring people to Nice unless they matter."

He nodded slowly. There was a part of him that felt honored. Another part… that wasn't sure if it was ready to matter again.

CHAPTER FORTY-THREE – GHOST ON THE GUEST LIST

Jennifer wasn't expecting to feel anything when she opened the speaker list. It was just another conference. Another keynote panel on inclusive policy design. Another chance to showcase her work and earn her next postdoc. She scrolled lazily, her eyes glazing over... until she saw it. "Sebastian Müller. Vanderbilt University / Real Madrid (formerly)." Her body froze, as if her heart had been yanked back into a place it never wanted to return to. It was the name. But more than that, it was seeing it next to her field. Development policy. AI in fiscal systems. Latin America. It wasn't a football article. It wasn't a tabloid. It was him, in her world.

The shock came first, and the deep impact came a bit later.

Then came the tremor under her ribs—a mix of anxiety and something she didn't want to call hope. She clicked the panel name. He was scheduled for Geneva on the same track as hers. Two panels apart. Same hallway. Same badge. It was happening. She tried to be rational, reminding herself that she had Felipe, a career, and a life. But her fingers shook as she typed "Sebastian Müller + Real Madrid" into Google.

The images hit hard. His face. Older. Sharper. Videos of goals. Celebrations. One... with a message written on a white undershirt:

"WHERE ARE YOU, J?"

Her breath caught. Another showed him gesturing a cursive

"J" in the air after scoring. Thousands of fans replicated it on TikTok. No one knew who it was for. But she did.

She dove deeper. The forums. The YouTube breakdowns. The Reddit threads are full of conspiracy theories. "Is Real Madrid's golden boy hiding a lost love?" "Müller's secret muse?"

She sat in her hotel room, the conference badge still around her neck, the laptop glowing in the dark. And for the first time in years... she felt like she didn't know what ground she was standing on anymore.

Meanwhile, in Rome, Sebastian was watching Camille adjust her knight on the chessboard in the third round of an international tournament. She looked devastatingly elegant, and he wanted to say no—to stay in Geneva. He wanted to try his search in the conference one more time. But she had called, whispered that she missed him, and said she had a "feeling" he needed a break.

And how could he say no to that voice? How could he keep chasing a ghost? He didn't know that Jennifer was preparing to surprise him. He didn't know that she had seen everything. He didn't know... that she was still watching.

Jennifer stood in the conference hall in Geneva as the panel began without him. His chair was empty. His name was crossed out. Someone else was presenting the paper he co-wrote. Her throat went dry. She stood the entire time, didn't ask a question, or blink. She walked out before the applause. She felt sick. And suddenly... more lost than ever.

CHAPTER FORTY-FOUR – SHIFTING GRAVITY

Felipe was leaving Paris. Jennifer knew it was coming. His visiting post had ended.

Chicago needed him back. The university. The students. The research center with his name on the door. He was a machine of quiet brilliance. She had always admired that about him. But now... she feared it.

They sat on a bench near the Seine on his last weekend. He held her hand like it was still easy.

Still whole.

"We could settle in Chicago," he said softly.

"There are fellowships. Positions. And it's... real, Jenn."

She smiled faintly. Didn't answer. Then he added, casually, dreamily:

"I'd love for us to start thinking about a family."

Her stomach turned. He had said it before. Months ago. After their "decade celebration." That night that broke something inside her, she never named. But now, it was clear: he meant it.

"I need to tell you something," she said.

He looked over, expectant. But her voice failed her.

"I just... I'm not ready."

He nodded, still warm. "That's okay. We don't have to rush."

But then—

"But you do want that. Eventually?"

That question broke her open in ways she didn't expect. That night, she didn't sleep. She didn't answer his messages. She just opened her laptop and typed his name again: "Sebastian Müller." From Madrid... to Nashville. MLS. Vanderbilt. Conferences. She built the timeline like a puzzle. He had been everywhere, and yet they never met. Maybe they weren't supposed to. Maybe they were just unfinished. She didn't tell Felipe she was tracking Sebastian. She barely told herself. But one thing became clear: before she could move forward... she had to close the past with truth, not silence.

Meanwhile, in Rome, Sebastian and Camille were doing well. She laughed easily and made bold moves in chess and life. She was there—everywhere. He wasn't sure it was love, but it was constant. Camille didn't ask permission to fit into his world; she simply did. When his contract required him to return to Nashville, she moved too, just like that. No drama, no hesitation.

"You're worth the miles," she said simply. And she meant it. They traveled for games, toured cities, and shared hotel rooms, coffee, and strategy books. It was easy, maybe too easy. But Sebastian had made peace with something: He hadn't found Jennifer. He had stopped looking.

Camille was brilliant, elegant, present, and not a ghost. He returned to the pitch for his MLS debut. Crowds, noise, but still: Academia first. That was the deal. That was his word. He played because he signed, and studied because he chose. Camille was proud. Everyone was watching. But somewhere deep in his chest, something still felt... out of sync.

CHAPTER FORTY-FIVE – THE ENDING BEFORE THE RETURN

The apartment in Paris felt hollow. Felipe had already returned to Chicago. He left behind a scarf, a half-full bottle of wine, and a voice message she still hadn't listened to. Jennifer stood by the window, fingers wrapped around a cup of tea that had gone cold two hours ago. She had typed and deleted the message at least fifteen times. And now... She finally knew what to say.

"Felipe,
I love the life we tried to build.
I love the silence we filled with brilliance.
I love the respect. The way you held me, not like possession, but like purpose.

But I can't give you a future if I'm still tied to a past I never let end properly.
You deserve someone who dreams with you, not someone still afraid to sleep.

I don't know where this road takes me.
But I know I need to walk it alone.

I'm sorry.
J."

She hit send. The phone slipped gently from her hand onto the couch, and her chest cracked wide open, not with grief, but with a release. She didn't cry—not yet.

Instead, she opened a map and searched quietly for Nashville.

Flight routes, short-term stays, and a conference schedule at Vanderbilt. She wasn't sure if she would see him or if he'd want to see her. But something inside her knew this had to end with words, not silence. She owed it to him, to herself, and to the ghost she had carried for far too long.

She packed light. Nothing dramatic. No fantasies. Just jeans, notes, a folder with a paper she never submitted — the one that started it all. The one she wrote the night after the miscarriage.

Kathe called.

"Where are you going?"

Jennifer paused. Then said softly:

"To breathe."

As the plane took off, she didn't rehearse what she'd say. She didn't even know if she'd say anything.

But this time... she wouldn't run away. Not from him. Not from what she lost. Not from what she still needed to understand.

In a city she'd never been to, with no guarantee of being received, Jennifer was finally coming to face the only chapter she never finished writing.

CHAPTER FORTY-SIX – THE ORIGIN OF THE QUIET MAN

Felipe Santos Ospina was born in a working-class neighborhood in Bogotá, not far from Jennifer's barrio. His surroundings were characterized by cracked concrete streets, tin roofs, and curtains made from repurposed tablecloths. He experienced a childhood where milk was measured by spoons and bread was broken into fours, not halves.

His father, Ramiro Santos, was a policeman—a quiet man, strict—and a man who stopped speaking like a human being sometime around 1989. That year, Ramiro's best friend, who also happened to be the husband of the aunt who raised Felipe, was killed during a mission against Pablo Escobar's sicarios. Ramiro survived, but he never really returned.

He requested discharge from the force, bought a beat-up taxi, and drove it in near silence for the better part of a decade. Felipe grew up under that shadow, not one of violence, but of emotional absence.

His mother, Norma, worked shifts at a textile factory. She washed clothes by hand on Sundays and slept less than anyone else in the house. Felipe had three younger brothers and an older sister.

But amid his father's absence and his mother's attention to his younger siblings, it was his aunt Alba who really raised him.

She was a high school teacher who was widowed before she turned thirty and never remarried. Jacobo was her first and only love, Ramiro's best friend since they started talking. Alba moved into Ramiro's house when Jacobo died to help them, to help herself. Although Jacobo died a hero, Alba carried her grief like others carry a handbag: without ever complaining, but always close at hand.

Felipe wasn't the brightest. Nor the loudest. But he was curious. And that saved him.

At fifteen, he got a job as a caddy at a golf club in northern Bogotá. Amid golf balls, green grass, and "¡Fore!", he met a girl who played tennis every afternoon: Marcela Barco. Tall. Elegant. Sharp. And she looked at him, not like a poor kid from the south, but like someone who had already seen what he could become.

Marcela used to say Felipe was like Harry Potter in his first year at Hogwarts— all the magic, none of the tools. She helped him with his homework, lent him books, and taught him how to use all the cutlery on the table. He made her laugh. It was an uneven love story, but never unfair. Felipe's brilliance wasn't imagined; it was just buried.

In his final year of high school, pressured by Aunt Alba, he took the national university exam. He placed third in the entire country. No one expected it—not even Marcela. Her father, Senator Pedro Barco, a seasoned liberal with a reputation for fairness, stepped in. Influenced by Marcela, he asked the best private university in the country, where he personally funded scholarships, to assign one to Felipe. And that's where it all began.

Felipe studied two degrees: Engineering and Economics. He gained efficient aspects of engineering and social and political insights from economics. The early semesters were brutal, but Marcela helped him through.

And Felipe rose, first among his classmates, then among his professors, and eventually into elite circles he never knew existed. He was set to graduate with honors, beside Marcela, with job offers and letters of recommendation—a future already written.

Until the accident, a drunk driver ran a red light. Their car flipped three times. Marcela died instantly. Felipe survived with a fractured leg and a few cuts, along with a wound no scan could reveal.

From that day on, his smile changed. Not because he couldn't smile, but because he knew joy could vanish in seconds. He dove into his career, his books, and his students. He became brilliant, gentle, and charismatic. He taught like someone who wanted to protect, and he listened like someone who had lost. To most people, Felipe was nearly perfect. But only Jennifer ever truly knew him. Only she had heard the truth about Marcela, the taxi, Aunt Alba, and what it meant to build a future out of the pieces of a broken dream.

Felipe wasn't a flawless portrait. He was a man of cracks, stitched together by discipline and empathy. And the only place he ever felt truly safe was at the other end of a voice note that ended in a quiet, familiar "muah."

CHAPTER FORTY-SEVEN – WHERE IT ALWAYS WAS

Jennifer stepped out of the taxi and into the warm air of Nashville. No cameras.

No script. Just breath and nerves and a quiet prayer she didn't know how to say out loud. The campus at Vanderbilt was vast and green, and its buildings were elegant yet understated.

Nothing screamed football or fame. But she wasn't looking for the player. She was looking for him. The boy who became a man in silence. Who learned to heal in motion.

She walked slowly through the quad, her bag slung over one shoulder and her hair tucked behind her ears. She didn't know what she was hoping for. Maybe just… a glance.

And then, it happened. At the center of the lawn, near the old oak tree, he was walking out of a lecture building, holding a notebook and looking down. She stopped. He looked up. Their eyes met. And time—stopped.

They didn't move. Not at first. Then he did. One step. Another. Faster. Like he didn't know whether to run or fall. His hand shook. His lips parted. His eyes refused to blink. And then—

He spoke first. "I'm sorry."

Not for what he did. But for everything he never had words for.

Jennifer felt the tears rising, hot and wild. She stepped closer. No hesitation. And whispered:

"Te amo."

Sebastian froze. Completely.

He stared at her like he feared she'd disappear if he breathed too hard. And then, softly—like air escaping from somewhere deep in his chest—he whispered:

"What do you mean?"

Jennifer smiled, her eyes wet, and said what Felipe once said to her:

"I never stopped. I just learned how to live without you."

His face cracked open. A smile. A sob. A thousand lifetimes in a second. He dropped his notebook. Held her face in both hands like she was made of glass and gravity.

They kissed. No music. No crowd. Just them. After everything. After everyone.

But not everyone had missed it. Across the street, Camille sat in the passenger seat of a parked car. She had arrived to pick him up. She saw him walking out. She saw the woman across the lawn. She saw their faces when they locked eyes. She didn't move. She didn't cry. She just placed a hand on her stomach, a stomach only barely starting to curve. Her lips pressed into a tight line. She had known this might happen. She didn't expect it to feel like this.

She didn't get out; she just pulled the door closed softly and waited. He would come, and he would tell her because Camille wasn't afraid of truth, not even when it came with heartbreak.

And as Jennifer held on to Sebastian under the Tennessee sun, she thought for the first time in years:

"This is where I was always going."

CHAPTER FORTY-EIGHT – THE THINGS WE DON'T SAY

Camille didn't cry in the car. She watched them from a distance—Sebastian and the woman she already knew was her.

Jennifer.

The name she had suspected for months. The ghost behind Sebastian's silences. The echo in his eyes when she laughed too loudly. The wall he never let her touch. Now the ghost had a face. A voice. Arms around his neck. And Camille finally knew:

She had never stood a chance.

She didn't storm in. Didn't scream. Didn't beg. She waited. Let them disappear into the building.

Let the street go quiet. Then, she turned the key in the ignition and drove. No music. No calls. Just the sound of her breath, steady and composed.

When Sebastian returned to the apartment that night, the lights were off.

The kitchen was clean. The books were stacked. Her favorite scarf was gone from the coat rack. On the desk was a single envelope. No name. Just one word:

"*Merci.*"

Inside, a handwritten note:

"You are beautiful.

You are brilliant.

But your heart was never here.

And mine deserves a place it can stay.

No need to write.

I've already said goodbye.

Camille."

By then, she was already in the air, on a flight to Nice, where her mother would be waiting.

Her old room still had posters on the wall—some with his face. The irony didn't sting anymore. She wasn't running; she was protecting. Not just herself... but someone else now, too.

She didn't plan to tell him— not now, not soon, maybe never. He didn't deserve to be punished with fatherhood or glorified with it. He had chosen his path; she would walk hers.

Back in Nashville, Sebastian stood in the doorway of the now-empty apartment.

Camille was gone.

No confrontation. No confession. Just absence. And in that silence, he felt something strange: Not guilt. But a clarity he hadn't felt in years. For the first time, there were no shadows left between him and Jennifer. No what-ifs. No debts. He felt... free. And maybe that was the most dangerous feeling of all.

CHAPTER FORTY-NINE – THE CHAPTER WE SKIPPED

They didn't tell anyone. Not at first. Not Felipe. Not Kathe. Not Camille. Not even Franz or the girls. Because the decision wasn't about logic.

It was about something faster. Something irrational. Something so intensely joyful it refused to wait for permission.

They were having coffee one morning. Still high off the reunion. Still tangled in bed sheets and half-finished poems on napkins.

And Sebastian said— "What if we never stopped being married?"

Jennifer blinked. "What do you mean?"

"We never really undid it," he shrugged. "I mean, yeah — paperwork. But not us."

She stared at him and then laughed. She did not mention that she had completely forgotten about him while in Felipe's arms.

"Are you saying we're still married by... default?"

He grinned. "No.

I'm saying we should go to Vegas this weekend and fix the paperwork."

They bought inexpensive tickets. They drove into the desert like fugitives fleeing their own history. They laughed too loudly. They got drunk on nostalgia and champagne. Then they married. Again. Same names. Same people. Just a different version of themselves. Wiser. Less afraid. Or so they believed.

It worked for months. They divided their time between Nashville and guest lectures in other cities. She began consulting for an international agency. He played his last MLS season with grace and no ego. They kissed in bookstores, held hands in lecture halls, and stayed in cheap motels just to feel like they were 20 again. It was happiness in its purest form. Or maybe... happiness in denial.

Until New York...

A layover. Winter air filled the terminal. Coffee in paper cups. Their luggage had already been checked for the flight back to Nashville. Jennifer wandered into a bookstore near Gate C13. She liked to read the magazines she'd never buy. That's when she saw it: the cover.

VOGUE Paris... Camille Moreau.

Hair slicked back. Perfect cheekbones. Holding a child. A baby with golden curls and pale blue eyes! Eyes she recognized. Sebastian's eyes.

The headline read:

"Model. Diplomat. Mother. Camille's Double Life in the French Riviera."

Jennifer didn't scream. She didn't move. The magazine slipped from her hand as she grabbed a bench.

Then everything went fuzzy. The floor came up too fast.

Sebastian turned the corner just in time to see her slump sideways, knees giving out, arms flailing toward nothing. He caught her. Passengers rushed by. A flight attendant called for help.

And as she blinked through the haze, she didn't say his name. She didn't say anything. She just pointed to the magazine... and

whispered:
   "Is that your child?"

CHAPTER FIFTY – THE ANSWER IN HIS EYES

The terminal was still buzzing, but all Sebastian heard was his heartbeat. Jennifer's question hadn't been a scream; it was a whisper—so quiet it might have been mistaken for disbelief, except for her eyes. Her eyes weren't whispering anything. "Is that your child?" She held the magazine as if it burned, her hand trembling, her voice unsteady but devastatingly calm. Sebastian didn't move, didn't blink, didn't breathe. Because in that instant... she knew.

She didn't need a yes. She had seen the baby's face. His mouth. His eyes. His little hand was clinging to Camille's sweater just like Sebastian used to cling to her shoulder when he slept on long flights.

He crouched in front of her on the airport floor, with passengers walking around them and announcements echoing above. He reached for her hand, but she pulled away slowly and quietly, like a retreat.

"I didn't know," he said.

Not defensive. Not desperate. Just shattered.

Jennifer looked at him like he was a stranger who had her wedding ring in his pocket.

"But you... could have known."

He nodded, swallowing hard. "I know."

"I saw her. She saw us," she whispered. "And she left. She let you go. She never told you."

"I swear, Jenn. I never—"

"I believe you."

Her voice cracked. "That's not the point."

He sat back on his heels, mouth open, hands loose.

"I never asked her if she was okay," he said softly. "I never asked what we were."

Jennifer stood. Shaky, but tall.

"That was a luxury you gave yourself."

The gate agent called final boarding. Neither of them moved.

He stared at the magazine still on the floor. The baby's face.

Camille's smile — serene, distant, untouchable. She had chosen silence. He had let her.

"I was yours," Jennifer said. "All in. Again."

Sebastian looked up. "I still am."

She paused.

"But I won't be the one who pays the price for something you never confronted."

She didn't cry. Not in that moment. But he did. Because for the first time since Rome, he realized: Camille had never truly left. She had simply waited for the right mirror. Jennifer picked up the magazine, folded it once, and then placed it gently on his lap. "Find out the truth."

She looked him in the eyes. "And then come find me."

She turned and walked toward the gate. She didn't look back; she didn't need to. He was already gone.

CHAPTER FIFTY-ONE – THE GARDEN WHERE SHE WAITS

Nice was quiet in late spring. Not silent. Not empty. Just intentional. Camille moved through her parents 'garden as if she belonged to it — barefoot, a robe draped over her body, her belly now soft and loose after birth, her hair still damp from the morning shower. The baby had just gone down for his nap. She had one hour — maybe two — of peace. She held a cup of rooibos tea in her hand, not for the caffeine, but for the ritual. She needed rituals now.

The house was the same one she had grown up in: bright, modern, filled with corners that held memories—some gentle, some sharp. Her mother didn't say much when Camille returned from Nashville without warning. She didn't have to. She opened the door, looked once at her daughter's face, and pulled her into the kind of hug that says you don't need to explain.

Camille hadn't planned on becoming a mother. Not then. Not like this. Yet once she saw the test, once she felt the truth growing inside her... she didn't hesitate. She wouldn't fight for him. Wouldn't beg for space in a man's life who had already drawn a new map.

She had always known how to walk away with grace.

Still, a part of her wondered if he'd call. If he'd ask. But weeks passed. Then months. Instead, she received a text from an old producer: "Saw you disappear. But I heard you're a mom now? Any interest in sharing that story?" Camille hesitated. She didn't want headlines. Or pity. But then she saw her son crawling across the rug for the first time, chasing a wooden giraffe with pure joy. And she thought:

"If the world's going to tell a story... I'd rather write it myself."

The photoshoot was simple: soft light, natural hair, and no designer clothes. Just Camille, barefoot in her garden, holding her son as he giggled into the breeze. The magazine called it:

"The Model Rewritten: Camille Moreau's Double Life."

They didn't mention Sebastian. She hadn't given them a name. But Jennifer didn't need one. Camille saw it in the analytics spike the day the cover went viral. Someone had searched. Someone had seen. She had lit the match. Now, all she had to do was wait for the smoke to rise.

Back in the garden, Camille rocked her son gently on the porch swing.

She whispered to him in French.

"Tu es mon soleil.""– You are my sun."

Not a mistake. Not a secret. Not a symbol of loss. But a new story. Hers.

CHAPTER FIFTY-TWO – WHAT WE CAN'T CARRY TOGETHER

They landed in Nashville like a couple returning from vacation. No one knew about the fainting spell. The magazine. The baby's eyes. They smiled at the taxi driver. Tipped well. Held hands as they walked into the apartment. But by the second night, silence had returned between them.

Not hostile. Not cold. Just… distant.

Like they were roommates in a house filled with memories.

Sebastian sat on the edge of the bed the next morning, staring at his phone. Jennifer stood in the hallway, watching him through the mirror. She knew what was coming. He turned to her, soft and careful. "I need to see him," he said.

She blinked once. Didn't move.

"I'm not going to France to build a family. "

"I just… I need to see if he's mine."

She sat down slowly, across from him. "You don't trust the photo?"

"I do," he said. "Too much. That's the problem."

He looked at her with glassy eyes.

"I'm not angry at her. I just— I deserve to know."

Jennifer nodded. Then whispered:

"And what do I deserve?"

He didn't answer.

Because anything he said would've sounded like a lie.

She stood up, slow and light, like a ghost lifting off the floor.

And in that moment, she wasn't the girl he kissed at the quad. She wasn't his Vegas wife. She was the woman who had tried twice to give him everything. And this time, she knew when to stop trying.

"I can't share you with this," she said. "I can't wait in silence while you fly to France chasing the truth I already saw in that child's eyes."

"I'll come back," he said.

She nodded. "I believe you. But not to me."

They didn't scream. No door slammed. Just two people realizing, slowly, painfully:

This was the limit.

And love, no matter how strong, could not erase a need for *truth* that wasn't hers to give or deny.

That night, she packed two bags. One for her clothes. The other for memories she didn't want to leave behind again.

Sebastian watched from the doorway, paralyzed.

She kissed his cheek once.

Pressed a hand over his heart.

"Don't come after me this time."

Her flight left at dawn for Bogotá. Her mother was sick, and her father was alone. She needed to reconnect with her roots. But more than anything, she needed to feel like she belonged to herself again.

CHAPTER FIFTY-THREE – THE DOOR THAT STAYED OPEN

Nice was quiet that morning. Sebastian stood in front of the gate, palms sweaty and heart heavy.

He had nothing in his hands—no gift, no flowers. Just the weight of too many silent months and a name he wasn't sure he had the right to say aloud:

"Camille."

He rang the bell and waited. He thought maybe she wouldn't answer, that someone else would come, and he'd feel like a stranger. But when the door opened—she was there. Calm, barefoot, wearing a linen shirt and a small gold chain, hair up, eyes unreadable.

They stood there for a moment. Then she stepped aside. No hug. Just space. "He's in the garden."

Sebastian walked slowly through the corridor. The house smelled of lavender and soap. Every corner felt warm. Lived-in. And then... There he was. On the grass. Tiny fingers wrapped around a plastic soccer ball. Giggling. Wobbling toward a tree. Curls bouncing. Eyes... His eyes...

Sebastian froze. Something in his chest collapsed and expanded at the same time. He didn't speak. He just dropped to one knee. And the boy, curious, toddled toward him without hesitation.

Put one chubby hand on his cheek. And smiled.

Sebastian choked back something that didn't have a name.

Camille watched from the patio. Didn't interrupt. Didn't speak.

Until he finally turned to her. Tears in his eyes.

"I... I didn't know love could be this small."

She smiled softly. "I did."

They sat together later on the porch, the baby now asleep.

Camille handed him a glass of water.

"I didn't tell you," she said, evenly, "because I didn't want to trap you."

"I wouldn't have felt trapped," he whispered.

She raised an eyebrow. Didn't challenge it. Just looked at the garden.

"I love you, you know," she said.
"Not for what you were. Or for the baby. But for how you looked at the world when you weren't pretending to be more than human."

He swallowed.

"I'm sorry."

"I know."

Then her voice changed. It was not cold, but steel wrapped in grace.

"You are his biological father. That's undeniable, but he is not your son in any legal or custodial sense. He carries my last name. He will know the truth when the truth can serve him. Not when it serves you."

Sebastian nodded slowly. "I want to be there. If he needs me."

Camille looked at him. Long. Steady.

"You can visit, you can know him. But you will not decide for him. You will not shape him. Unless, someday... he asks for you."

There was no malice in her tone. No spite. Just dignity.

That unmistakable French elegance could say no without raising its voice. She stood.

"I don't expect anything from you. I don't need anything. And I don't want you back."

He looked up, startled. She smiled.

"I love you, Sebastian. That's not a door I plan to close with bitterness. But love... doesn't mean return. It just means recognition."

He stood too. And as he turned to leave, she whispered

"He likes to sleep with music. The same song every night."

"What song?"

She paused and then smiled sadly. "The one you hummed every time you tied your cleats."

He blinked.

"Camille...". But she just kissed his cheek and went back inside.

CHAPTER FIFTY-FOUR – THE SPACE THAT GRIEF LEAVES BEHIND

Bogotá felt colder than she remembered. Not in terms of the weather, though the drizzle seemed permanent, but in the sensation of walking streets that once held her childhood and now only reflected her grief.

Her father picked her up at the airport. He had aged. Not in years, but in something heavier.

It was as if the house had grown quieter without her mother, and he didn't know how to fill the silence.

Her mother was already sick when Jennifer arrived. But still herself. Still folding napkins into little birds. Still insisting on brushing her hair, still whispering, "*te veo cansada,*" even when Jenn hadn't spoken.

She endured for three weeks. One night, her fever spiked. Her breath rattled.

And the space that held her love simply... emptied.

The funeral was small, attended by relatives, neighbors, and a few friends Jennifer hadn't seen in years. At the back of the chapel stood one stranger in a black coat. She caught a glimpse of him from the side, eyes low, head bowed. Felipe. He didn't approach or speak; he just remained there, like a statue, like a lighthouse in the fog.

Jennifer didn't cry until hours later, sitting on the kitchen floor, clutching her mother's scarf.

That's when the tears came, loud and reckless. And for the first time since she'd arrived, she whispered— "I have no one."

Her father cooked less, stopped watching *fútbol*, and mostly listened silently to the radio. Jennifer tried to write, to teach, to apply. But she was in limbo. Not quite Bogotá. Not quite anywhere. She wasn't a daughter anymore, a wife, or a professor —just a ghost in her own hometown.

The newspaper obituary was brief. Felipe had accidentally seen it while sipping coffee at his desk in Chicago.

And the moment he read the name "Olga López de González", his breath caught.

He booked a flight that same day. Stood at the funeral. Said nothing. But he stayed until the last person left. And then... He disappeared again.

A month later, Jennifer found an envelope under the apartment door.

No name. Just a card.

"Duelo no es olvido.

Te acompaño desde la distancia."

– F.

She held it to her chest. Didn't respond. Not then.

Weeks turned to months. The days blurred into gray. Until one afternoon, on her birthday, a message lit up her phone.

Felipe: "I know it's not a happy birthday.

But you're still here.

And I'm still here, if you need a north star."

She stared at it for a long time. Then replied:

"Sometimes I don't even know which direction is north."

And he answered—

"That's what stars are for."

They didn't talk every day, but when they did, his words came like medicine—slow, grounding. He never asked what happened with Sebastian, never pressed, never compared. He just listened. And when she didn't want to talk, he simply stayed on the line, breathing, present. And slowly... Ever so slowly... Jennifer began to return to herself. Not as before. But new. More tender. More tired. But still standing.

CHAPTER FIFTY-FIVE
– THE QUIET GAME

Sebastian walked off the plane in Newark feeling both heavier and lighter than when he had boarded in Nice. He hadn't cried when he left Camille's house. He hadn't kissed the baby goodbye. He simply looked at him one last time, memorizing the shape of his tiny hand wrapped around a spoon. There were no promises. No drama. Just a truth they both carried now. He was a father. And yet... he wasn't.

Back in Nashville, the apartment was quiet. Jennifer's absence felt more final than ever before. Not like a breakup—more like an eviction from a dream. He didn't sleep that night; he just sat on the floor and stared at a photo of their wedding in Vegas.

Two fools. Two hearts desperate to rewrite the past.

He smiled, then cried, then smiled again. The next morning, he went to campus. No press. No press conference. No training. Just coffee, a chalkboard, and students who barely recognized his name anymore. He guest-lectured that afternoon, not about economics but about decision-making under uncertainty. And for the first time in weeks, he felt useful.

In the months that followed, Sebastian stayed put. No transfers. No interviews. No press junkets. He played one final MLS game — his contract fulfilled — and then quietly retired. He left with no farewell post, no video montage, just a pair of worn-out boots in a donation bin near the locker room door.

He resumed publishing papers, focusing on behavioral economics, policy and performance under pressure, and using sport as a framework for decision design. He presented at conferences where no one asked him for a selfie, and it was... peaceful.

Sometimes he checked Camille's social media from a burner account. The baby was growing fast. His smile was radiant. His legs strong. Sebastian never messaged. Never liked. Just watched. From a respectful, aching distance.

Jennifer never called. And he didn't blame her. He had made too many quiet choices. And silence, eventually, makes its own bed.

One night, while returning from a lecture, he saw a kid juggling a soccer ball under a streetlamp. The boy was maybe nine, with messy hair (and a Messi jersey) and no shoes.

Sebastian stopped and watched, then stepped closer. "Can I try?" he asked.

The kid shrugged, and they passed the ball for ten minutes.

Then the boy asked, "Were you a player?"

Sebastian smiled. "Something like that."

That night, he wrote the first lines of his new book. Not a memoir. Not a confession. Just a guide.

"This isn't a book about what I won.

It's about what I learned when I stopped needing to win."

CHAPTER FIFTY-SIX – CONVERGENCE IN WASHINGTON DC

Jennifer

IMF Headquarters 1 – Washington, D.C.

Jennifer waited quietly, her knees gently pressed together, the soft noise of the IMF hallway settling like a silent heartbeat around her. The morning sun filtered through the large windows, casting long golden lines across the marble floor. She wasn't nervous, not like she used to be. She was focused, calm in a way that only comes when everything has fallen apart and you've learned to pull yourself together.

A year ago, she could barely leave her apartment without shaking. Now she sat here, dressed in a simple navy blue suit, her hands folded loosely over a leather briefcase containing her notes and something much more fragile: her hope. Her mother's voice echoed softly in her thoughts: "Be brave, mija. Don't worry, no one dies on the eve of a big day." Be brave. She was. She is.

She glanced at the silver watch on her wrist. It had belonged to her mother. It no longer ticked, but it didn't matter: time had already broken once when her mother died, and she had sewn it back together. It wasn't perfect, but it was hers.

She breathed slowly, calming her pulse. Each breath reminded her that she was no longer hiding from life. She had studied for this. She had earned it. Global markets, climate finance, fiscal response frameworks... It was all in her head, it was all part of who she was now. She was ready.

As she looked around, her eyes caught movement in the glass-walled meeting room. A tall man stood near the back wall, half turned, looking at something on his phone. The curve of his shoulders. The slight tilt of his head. For a second, just a second, she caught her breath. Felipe?

She almost smiled, not with joy, but with disbelief at her own imagination. Of course not, she thought. Felipe worked at the World Bank, not here. Still... her gaze lingered. Once he had stood there like that, hands in his pockets, watching her silently before speaking.

For a moment, her chest ached. The last time she had seen him was at her mother's funeral. He had appeared like a shadow and held her when she could no longer stand. They hadn't spoken since then. The distance. The grief. Life. And yet, in her most intimate moments, she still felt his presence, like a gentle wind behind her as she moved forward, helping her stay afloat.

The figure moved and disappeared behind a column. She let the image slip away.

An employee came out into the hallway and called her name. Now. She stood up straight, smoothed her skirt, and greeted him with a slight nod. One last look at the room: the man was gone.

She walked forward, her mother's watch catching the light, her heart steady. She was no longer the Jennifer who left Bogotá. She was no longer the Jennifer who hid in Barcelona. She was something new. Something she didn't even know she could become.

And if fate was real—and she was beginning to think that perhaps it was—then this city was about to bring all the threads of her story back together.

She didn't look back. Not yet.

Felipe

World Bank Main Complex – Washington, D.C.

Felipe leaned against the window on the ninth floor of the World Bank, his forehead almost touching the cold glass. From that distance, he could barely make out the edge of the IMF building, all steel lines and white columns bathed in the morning sun. A small part of him whispered that this was foolish, but he stood there anyway, still, watching.

He knew he was there because a colleague had mentioned a brilliant Colombian woman with an impressive track record in a final interview.

That morning, he stopped by the IMF under the pretext of a meeting with colleagues, hoping—without saying it out loud—to see Jennifer. And he saw her, just for a second. She was sitting in the waiting room, her back straight, her hands folded calmly, her mother's watch peeking out from under her sleeve.

She looked... luminous. Not in appearance. In something else. In strength. And she looked beautiful.

He had seen her break down and rebuild herself. And now, she was exactly where she had once told him she dreamed of being.

He gently pressed his palm against the window. Not to reach her. Just to feel something.

He found himself thinking about the first time they met. She had been intense, brilliant, reserved ever since...

He had never told her clearly enough how he felt about her and how much he loved her. He hadn't told her because he wanted to protect her from a future that might never come. Because, deep down, he knew that their time together might not last as long as he wanted it to.

A soft chime broke the silence. He looked at the screen. An internal message. He furrowed his brow. He smiled—a tired, knowing smile—and went back to work. Let the city move. Let the threads move. Whatever it was, it wasn't finished yet. He didn't want to be seen then.

Sebastian

Just outside the World Bank, Washington, D.C., 19th Street and H Street.

Sebastian stepped out into the sunlight, the autumn breeze tugging gently at his jacket as he descended the last granite step of the World Bank. His folder with the interview material seemed thinner than before, as if it had already been committed to memory. He took a deep breath. It was done.

He walked aimlessly, the kind of walk that happens when the city itself feels charged. He hadn't been in D.C. since that DC United game Jenn took him to, weeks before he saw the magazine with Camille on the cover. But the air was the same: heavy with ambition, light with diplomacy. And somewhere beneath it all, a whisper of memory.

Her name came before the thought:

Jennifer.

He didn't know why she came to mind. Maybe it was the way the light hit the IMF building across the street. Maybe it was the quiet moment in the interview room when he was asked what kind of economist he hoped to be, and he remembered how she used to talk about changing the world as if it were a duty, not a dream.

He stopped at the corner of 19th and H, watching a group of workers laugh as they left the IMF. He smiled faintly. She would have fit in perfectly: studious, elegant, untouchable, and yet the most real person in the room.

They hadn't spoken in months. Their story had unfolded in whispers, lost time, and promises neither of them dared to make. She remembered the last message she wrote but never sent. After her mother's death, she wrote it a dozen times and deleted it every time.

And now she was here, on the same block, breathing the same air.

What were the odds?

She sat down on a bench between two cherry trees, the last pink petals falling like soft punctuation marks. The IMF building loomed just ahead. That same night, she had a flight back home, to a city that suddenly seemed farther away than ever.

If he got the scholarship, he would move here. Forever. Maybe fate was drawing him a map, not a perfect one, but one that curved gently toward places he thought he had left behind.

On a whim, she unlocked her phone and searched. Her name was still there, in an inactive thread: Jennifer A. She stared at it for a long time, her thumb hovering over the screen. Her heart gave a little jolt.

She didn't want to write anything heavy. Just... open the door.

"Hi Jen, I'm in DC for work. I know it's been months... I'd love to catch up if you're up for it. If not, I totally understand. Take care."

He hit send before he could change his mind.

And then... he breathed.

She might never reply. Maybe she had moved on; maybe her world had no room for old ghosts. But that wasn't the point.

The point was that he had said something.

At that moment, he received a notification, not from her, but from the scholarship coordinator. His heart skipped a beat. He replied.

"Hi, Sebastian? We have good news..."

He smiled as they talked. He had done it. The scholarship. The job. The new beginning.

Across the street, a woman was leaving the IMF building, her posture firm and her gait graceful. He didn't see her. But the moment... was near.

Jennifer. Sebastian. Felipe.

Three names suspended in the air above D.C., circling silently in the same sky.

Something was happening.

They couldn't see it yet. But history already knew.

CHAPTER FIFTY-SEVEN – WHERE THE SOUL FINDS SHELTER

Days later, the late afternoon breeze in Dupont Circle carried the early touch of fall — that gentle, almost imperceptible shift that made the city feel like it was exhaling.

Jennifer walked with purpose, her steps steady, though her hands still trembled slightly. The interview at the IMF was behind her now; she was on her first day of work, her first training, and she had done well. She had been sharp, thoughtful, and real herself. But the adrenaline still coursed through her veins. She glanced at her reflection in shop windows as she passed — not out of vanity, but disbelief. Am I really here? Did I really make it back?

Now, she was headed to meet Felipe, who had contacted her days before, after the interview. Their old café was tucked away on the corner of the square, small iron tables spilling out onto the sidewalk. And there he was — as always — a quiet figure in a crisp shirt, glasses low on his nose, forehead faintly creased as he read—something caught in her chest at the sight of him.

Neither of them saw the figure across the street. Standing at the edge of Q Street, Sebastian had been walking toward Farragut North when he noticed her—or thought he did.

At first, he assumed it was just a resemblance. But then he recognized her walk: the subtle way her hand tucked a strand of hair behind her ear. Jennifer. His pulse picked up. He hadn't seen her since everything fell apart. Since Nice. Since Nashville. Since Bogotá. She looked... good. Strong. Not the broken woman he had left behind.

Without thinking, his steps followed hers—not urgently, not invasively, just... drawn. She walked into the café. He slowed his pace and lingered on the other side of the street, eyes narrowed.

Inside, Jennifer saw Felipe and didn't hesitate. She walked straight to him, dropped her bag by the chair, and wrapped her arms around him.

He stood up, startled for a moment, before tightly closing his arms around her. She tucked her head into his chest like she used to. For a few seconds, the world paused.

Then she looked up and smiled through nerves and quiet relief. She kissed him, a soft, lingering press of lips to cheek.

—"It went well," she whispered. "But I was scared, Feli. Really scared."

He didn't say anything at first. Just stroked her arm, anchoring her.

—"It's over now," he said softly. "And you did it. I'm so proud of you, Jenny."

Her breath shook with release. That was all she needed.

Across the street, Sebastian stood frozen. He couldn't hear a word, but he didn't need to. He saw the hug, the kiss, and how she leaned into him.

And something inside him softened—not shattered, not flared with jealousy—just... shifted. She had found her home. And he was not it.

He exhaled slowly, then smiled—a small one, sad but sincere. He turned and walked away.

Back inside, Jennifer's voice bubbled with details. Felipe smiled, listening and watching her return to life in real time. But when she glanced down at her tea, he looked out the window. In that exact second, his eyes found Sebastian, standing across the street.

He saw him. Of course he did.

Saw the hesitation. The ache. The smile before the retreat. Felipe said nothing. Not now. Not yet.

He tucked the sight deep in his chest, where only he could feel its weight.

CHAPTER FIFTY-EIGHT – A CITY TOO SMALL

Washington, D.C. was many things — powerful, polished, historic. But to Sebastian, it felt mostly small, not in size, but in its circles. The deeper you went into global policy, elite economics, and international missions, the tighter the loop became.

It didn't take long for him to know exactly where she lived. He didn't seek it out. The city revealed it to him. Jennifer. With Felipe.

Three blocks from his apartment in Adams Morgan. Not hidden. Not flaunted. Just... there.

He didn't pass by on purpose, but he saw them on Sundays during morning coffee runs or quick walks to the bookstore on Connecticut.

She smiled. He carried the bags.

Once, Sebastian saw Felipe playing soccer in Cardozo — slow, out of breath, laughing too loudly for someone who couldn't trap the ball cleanly.

Sebastian stood on the opposite field, lacing his boots. No one there knew his name, just that he was ridiculously good. He didn't play to impress; he played to remember what it felt like to move without pressure: one pass, one run, one shot — all muscle memory. Sometimes a crowd gathered, people filming on their phones, but he ignored them all.

During the week, he was back in the World Bank loop— policy briefings, country visits, and field missions. Burkina Faso. Jakarta. Lima. Rabat. His passport filled up again. He sat with ministers, designed economic recovery plans, and talked about resilience as if it were a currency.

But D.C. was always the home base. Sometimes, he'd feel that knot in his stomach when walking home past the park.

"What if I turn the corner and see her?"

Sometimes he thought he did. A laugh behind him. A profile reflected in a shop window.

He never chased it. Never crossed the street.

He visited Nice a few times — not often. Enough.

Camille welcomed him politely. No tension. No hope.

Just a quiet arrangement. He saw the boy. Played with him. Held him until his arms hurt from not letting go. The boy called him "Seba." That was enough.

He never asked for more.

One night, after a flight from Nairobi, Sebastian sat on the rooftop of his building, the city blinking below.

He could see the block where they lived. He imagined them eating. Laughing. Maybe arguing over the news. He didn't hate Felipe. In fact, he respected him.

But when he saw him on the pitch — puffing, tripping over the ball, joking in terrible English— Sebastian couldn't help but think:

"She really chose that?"

Then he'd remind himself:

"She chose peace. And I'm not at peace."

He returned to juggling the ball in fields where no one asked questions, where no one knew he was once Real Madrid's number 27. Where no one remembered the viral celebration, he didn't need them to. Sometimes, it felt better to be anonymous than to simply be a guy who could still play.

CHAPTER FIFTY-NINE – WHAT WE OWE EACH OTHER

The evening was soft, the kind of quiet only Washington could produce after a long rain, where the city pulsed but the streets whispered. Jennifer came home to the scent of ginger tea and the low hum of Carlos Vives playing in the background.

Felipe was on the couch, a stack of folders on the coffee table, untouched. He smiled at her, but something about the curve of his lips felt thinner tonight. She leaned down to kiss his cheek. — "Tired?" she asked.

He nodded. Too quickly.

Something in her chest pulled tight. She sat beside him and waited. He looked at her for a long time and then took her hand. His voice was low and cracked at the edges: "I went to the doctor again today."

Jennifer turned slowly toward him. The room shifted. — "And?" she whispered.

Felipe swallowed hard. "The clock -he said- is ticking at the base of my neck. That's what the doctor said. Like poetry. Like cruelty."

Silence.

Only the rain began again on the window. He kept going, softly. "It's not aggressive yet. But it will be. Neurological. Inoperable."

Jennifer couldn't speak. He squeezed her hand tighter. "I wanted to wait until your job is settled. Until we were stronger. Until it wasn't raining. I don't know."

His smile was broken now. "I've tried to give you everything. Stability. Peace. Touch when you needed it, silence when you didn't. I know I pushed you once... about having a family." She flinched.

He noticed. "But now I realize... maybe fate stepped in. Maybe it saved you from raising a child with someone who wouldn't live long enough to help raise them."

His voice cracked. "I wanted that. I wanted to see our child grow. But not if it meant leaving you with all that weight."

Jennifer's eyes filled. Not just with tears. But with history. With everything she'd never said. She turned toward him fully now. Her voice was steady, but her fingers trembled.

"There was a time... where I did have that weight. You didn't know."

Felipe looked up. Still. Listening. Jennifer took a breath, one she didn't know she'd been holding for ten years.

"I was pregnant. Years ago. With your child."

He froze. Time stopped.

"I didn't know how to tell you. I was scared. I lost it before I ever said a word." The tears finally spilled.

"You would've been a wonderful father. And I... I didn't let you be. I robbed you of that. Not out of cruelty, but cowardice."

Felipe didn't interrupt. Didn't move. His hand reached out, brushing a strand of hair behind her ear. "You weren't a coward," he said. "You were in pain. And alone. That's not the same."

She shook her head. "I know now... because I saw the same happen to someone else." He tilted his head. Jennifer wiped her cheeks.

"Camille kept the baby from Sebastian. Just like I did with you." The room quieted again, and then Felipe did something she didn't expect.

He laughed. Soft. Shaky. "So we were always... hiding things from the only people who ever would've understood."

She rested her head on his chest.

He kissed the crown of her head. "I don't blame you," he whispered. "I blame time. And fear. And whatever cruel sense of humor the universe has."

They sat there for a long while. No more confessions. Just the sound of the rain. And a closeness that came from finally seeing each other altogether.

CHAPTER SIXTY – THE MAN ON BOTH SIDES

The email came without fanfare. Just a quiet note in Sebastian's inbox one morning:

"Sebastian,

I'd like to speak, if you're willing.

There's no agenda. Just something overdue.

— F."

No last name. No explanation. But Sebastian knew.

And strangely... he said yes. They met at a quiet café in Mount Pleasant: neutral ground, nothing dramatic. Felipe arrived first. He looked thinner, paler. The hands that once held markers and cue cards at conferences now held a cane; an old knee injury had reappeared, perhaps as a result of the treatment he was undergoing. Sebastian paused at the door when he saw him through the glass, not out of fear but out of confusion.

"Why now?"

He stepped in. "Felipe," he said softly.

Felipe smiled. "It's been a long time."

They shook hands. The kind of handshake two men give when neither knows if this will be the last.

The first meeting felt stiff, filled with surface pleasantries and discussions about books, soccer, and World Bank projects, yet there was no mention of her. The second meeting proved better, longer, and marked by more laughter.

Felipe's voice trembled when he spoke about his condition, but it never wavered when he mentioned Jennifer.

"She saved me," he said, simply. "By not asking me to be more than I could be."

Sebastian stared at the man across from him—the former professor, the ghost in Jennifer's arms, the shadow he'd tried to outrun. Something strange happened; he liked him.

The third time they met, Felipe said:

"There was never a competition, Sebastian. But if there was... I lost a long time ago."

Sebastian shook his head.

"No," he said. "If there was, I lost before it even started."

Felipe smiled.

"Maybe we both won. In the ways we were meant to."

By the fourth meeting, Sebastian was asking him questions about life, teaching, and the silence between people. In one quiet moment, he said, "You remind me of my brother."

Felipe raised an eyebrow. "Older brother?"

Sebastian nodded. "He stopped playing football after an injury. He still coaches. Still loves the game. But I never understood him... until now."

Felipe said nothing; he simply placed a hand on Sebastian's shoulder, and in that gesture, Sebastian forgave him—and perhaps, himself.

Felipe didn't inform Jennifer about the meetings. He didn't seek permission. He simply invited Sebastian to a small, cozy rooftop on U Street one evening and said:

"She'll be here. She doesn't know. Don't expect anything. Just listen."

When Jennifer arrived, she was carrying a tray of pastries from Tatte (her favorite place) and humming something from her childhood. She froze when she saw Sebastian, sitting under the string lights, looking both nervous and entirely at peace.

"You..." she started.

He stood up quickly. "I didn't know how to say no to him," Sebastian said with a naïve smile.

She laughed, unsure whether to cry or hug him. Instead, she sat. They talked—not about Nice, not about Nashville, not even about the baby—just about books, soccer, and how absurd it was that this city never really let anyone go.

For a moment, it felt as if nothing had ever broken. It was like they were two friends who had just drifted apart for a while and returned to the same bench. And in a way... that's exactly what they had become.

Somewhere behind them, watching from a neighboring rooftop, Felipe sipped bubble tea. Alone. Smiling. He didn't need thanks; he just needed to know they were both going to be okay.

CHAPTER SIXTY-ONE – WHAT WE LEAVE IN THE LIGHT

In Jenn And Felipe's Home

Jennifer opened her laptop just after dawn. The city was still asleep—even Felipe, curled softly on the couch, the blanket rising with every careful breath. She hadn't written like this in years. Not professionally. Not passionately. But now… the words poured out of her like water through a cracked dam.

An op-ed for the IMF. A paper on post-crisis institutional resilience. And then something else, unplanned—a memoir in fragments.

"Love has chapters. Some long. Some footnotes.
But every page matters."

She didn't write it for anyone; however, it was somehow meant for everyone. Felipe's illness had crept up on him. It didn't roar; it eroded. Sometimes, he forgot the street's name or poured milk twice into his coffee. But he was crystal clear on other days, especially when he watched her teach again. He came to one of her lectures at Georgetown and sat in the back. Tears welled in his eyes when she quoted one of his early research papers. She didn't even notice she'd done it.

That night, she told him:

"I think I'm ready to start saying yes again."

He nodded, knowing she meant to live, not just her career. And that was enough. But she also meant she wanted to start a family with him.

In Sebastian's Home

While he was watching Netflix, a message from Camille popped up on his phone:

"There will be a fashion show in D.C. It will be nothing flashy; it is just part of an NGO campaign about women and work. Do you mind taking care of Jonas?"

A few days later, Camille arrived with her usual, effortless poise — all French linen and soft command. Her hair was longer now. Her eyes were tired, but bright. A small boy with wild curls, wide eyes, and a Real Madrid backpack and a Jersey with "#29 Muller" in the back came with her.

Sebastian followed behind, quieter than usual and more grounded. He was amazed by the little one, who kept asking him questions in clear English with a strong French accent.

Sebastian's apartment is small and cozy. When the kid settled his bags and toys, Camille stepped forward and handed Bastian a folded drawing.

"He made this," she said.

It was a picture. Crude, childlike. A man. A ball. A bright sun overhead.

Sebastian blinked. "Is that me?"

Camille smiled.

"He's been hearing about you for a while. He loves your song, your poster, and all about you. I bought dozens of your jerseys; thank God they were on clearance because he only wants to be dressed in them."

Minutes later, when Camille left for her event, Sebastian took the kid to Jenn's home. He hadn't told Jennifer he planned to bring the boy. He just… felt it was time.

When the child entered their home, Felipe's face lit up with something Jennifer hadn't seen in weeks — a spark. Not just joy, but wonder. The boy initially clung to Jenn's leg, but gradually loosened his grip when Felipe offered juice and Sebastian pulled a tiny soccer ball from his schoolbag. Then, Felipe sat up straighter on the couch and opened his arms.

"Can I?" Sebastian nodded.

And the child climbed into his lap.

They didn't need introductions. Felipe looked into his face and saw all the chaos and grace of the lives that had orbited him. He smiled.

"You've got the legs of a midfielder," he said softly.

The boy grinned, not fully understanding, but comforted by the softness in Felipe's voice.

Camille came to Jenn's home that night when the event was over. They talked and laughed.

In a flash, Jennifer and Camille headed to the kitchen for some water and wine. They paused momentarily, observing the three of them — Felipe, the boy, and Sebastian, kneeling beside the couch.

Two women who had lost the same man in different ways stood together, and still... here they were. There was no jealousy, no tension, just life unfolding. Right.

That same night, after they had left, Felipe was still holding a toy that Jonas had forgotten at his house.

Jennifer lay down beside him. Felipe kissed her. That night they made love on the sofa. Still naked, shortly after they had fallen asleep, he whispered, "Do you know what I want more than anything?"

She nodded.

"To fall asleep one day and for everyone to go on with their lives."

She pressed her forehead against his. "We will. I promise."

Although the disease did not disappear, the treatment worked and allowed him to lead a practically normal life. Every now and then, Felipe complained of headaches or random dizziness, nothing out of the ordinary. However, a few days later and to the surprise of everyone, including his doctors, a heart attack took his life while he was getting dressed after a shower.

CHAPTER SIXTY-TWO
– HIS LAST DRAFT

Jenn's Home

The days after Felipe's funeral blurred into a long, soft silence.

Jennifer stayed mostly in their small apartment in Adams Morgan, curtains drawn against the spring light, clutching a mug of coffee she never finished. Sebastian visited every day. Sometimes they spoke, sometimes they didn't. He just sat beside her, a silent guardian, like a mountain unmoved by her storms.

A week after the funeral, an envelope arrived.

Handwritten. Heavy. Final.

Jennifer recognized Felipe's meticulous handwriting instantly. She sat on the worn couch, trembling fingers tracing the edges. Sebastian noticed and quietly sat beside her.

"Do you want me to stay?" he asked.

She nodded, swallowing back the lump in her throat. She opened the envelope carefully, as if afraid it might shatter.

"If you're reading this," it began,

"I have either died peacefully, or dramatically — in which case, forgive the timing of this letter. You know me, always late with drafts."

Jennifer let out a shaky laugh. Sebastian looked down, lips pressed together.

"I don't write this to say goodbye — I hope I did that in person, in my own quiet ways.

I write this to say that I saw you both. Entirely.

And I leave with no regrets.
None.
Not even the ones I once thought I'd carry to the grave.
  Jennifer…
You gave me a version of love I didn't think I deserved.
I know you've carried pain you never voiced, and still, you stayed kind.
You remained strong.
Your strength was never loud — it was steady, like ocean tides.
I loved you deeply.
And I let you go quietly, even while I was still holding your hand.
You don't owe me sadness.
You owe me legacy.
Keep building. Keep teaching. Keep being the light you are.
Every story I ever wanted to live had your name on it.
You were — and will always be — my Wonderwall."

  Jennifer covered her mouth with her hand. Tears fell freely.
Sebastian stepped closer.
  She kept reading.
  "Sebastian…
My almost-rival, my eventual student, my silent friend.
You are not what people say you are.
You are better.
I saw how you looked at the world — like it was something to win and also something to understand.
You played life like the game you knew best: one pass at a time.
I hope you raise your son knowing he has two names behind him
—
One that plays.
And one that teaches.
Both are worth honoring."

  Sebastian closed his eyes, letting the words settle like ash on water.
  "And to both of you…
I know what this looks like.
A strange triangle. A strange life.

But I don't believe in coincidence.
I believe in timing.
I believe you still have something to give each other —
Not romance, maybe.
Not an obligation.
But something bigger:
Truth.
The kind only people who've walked through fire together can carry.
The kind that saves someone else, someday."

At the bottom, there was no signature.

Just a line of his favorite quote, one he had written in Jennifer's notebook years ago:

"Love is not possession. It is preservation."

CHAPTER SIXTY-THREE – THE FINAL YES

Weeks passed.

Jennifer slowly returned to work, trying to reclaim fragments of her old self. But she felt strange, exhausted, and nauseous in the mornings. She blamed the grief, as everyone told her it would come in waves.

One afternoon, while editing a document, her vision swam. Everything tilted, and darkness swallowed the edges of her mind.

She fainted.

At the clinic, Sebastian waited, pacing like a lion in a too-small cage. When the doctor emerged, smiling broadly, Sebastian's heart dropped.

"Congratulations!" the doctor beamed. "Everything looks fine. She's just experiencing early pregnancy symptoms."

Sebastian froze. "Pregnancy?"

He looked into the examination room through the glass. Jennifer was sitting up, pale and confused, clutching a bottle of water like a life raft.

The doctor patted his shoulder warmly. "You're going to be a father. Get ready."

Sebastian swallowed, nodded politely, and went inside.

Jennifer's eyes locked onto his, wild and afraid.

"I'm pregnant," she whispered, as if afraid to speak the truth.

He sat beside her, took her hand. "It's okay," he said softly.

More than okay. It was life.

Tears welled in her eyes.

"I didn't even know... I can't tell him. I can't tell Felipe."

Sebastian tightened his grip. "You don't have to tell him," he said. "He already knew. He always knew you were carrying something beautiful."

They cried together — for loss, for life, for the impossible intertwining of both.

The months that followed were unlike anything Jennifer had known. Sebastian became her shadow:

- Driving her to appointments.
- Satisfying her cravings at 3 AM.
- Sitting with her through panic attacks when she feared losing the baby too.
- Laughing with her when hormones made her rage about the silliest things.
- Holding her when memories ambushed her without warning.

They weren't lovers. They weren't pretending. They were something deeper — partners in grief, co-parents by fate, friends stitched together by all the things they couldn't fix but could survive.

When the baby was born — a perfect boy with Felipe's serious eyes — Sebastian was there, holding her hand, whispering encouragement.

Jennifer named him Luis Felipe.

After his father. After the man who had believed in her even when she didn't.

They moved into a modest apartment in Adams Morgan — exposed brick, plants on the windowsill, a framed drawing from a boy in Nice on the kitchen wall.

Two months later, Jennifer and Sebastian were pushing the baby stroller down Massachusetts Avenue one spring evening. They weren't rushing anywhere. The world had slowed in a way Jennifer had once feared but now loved.

They paused in front of St. Matthew's Cathedral.

Jennifer looked up at the facade, caught his gaze, and smiled shyly.

"Maybe..." Sebastian said, voice thick with emotion, "Maybe we should get married. Properly this time. Church. Vows. Family. The whole crazy thing."

Jennifer's breath caught. Tears brimmed at the corners of her eyes. She leaned in, kissed him — a soft, sure kiss. When she pulled back, she whispered:

"That's your 'I do 'once again, Sebastian."

And the bells of St. Matthew's rang out overhead. Not an ending. Not a beginning. A continuation.

CHAPTER SIXTY-FOUR – AND THEN, EVERYTHING MADE SENSE

One evening, sitting on their battered old couch, Jennifer looked up from feeding little Felipe Andrés and said:

"We should do it before the year ends."

Sebastian, who had a soccer ball balanced on his head to make Jonas laugh, let it fall and caught it expertly.

"Do what?" he teased.

She smiled — the small, secret smile he loved most.

"Get married. Properly. Church. Family. Friends. Before life throws us something else."

Sebastian stood up, handed Jonas the ball, and crossed the room.

He knelt — no ring, no grand speech — just pure Sebastian: raw and real.

"Jennifer Alexandra González López... will you marry me — again, properly, before the city changes its mind?"

She laughed, tears rushing to her eyes. Jonas clapped without knowing why. The baby gurgled in approval.

"Yes," she whispered.

And this time, it wasn't rushed. It wasn't forced. It wasn't survival. It was a choice.

The bells of Saint Matthew's Cathedral rang clearly over Washington, D.C., catching in the late summer air and drifting down over the streets like music from another time. Inside, the cathedral glowed with golden light. Tall arches framed the altar. Candles flickered. A quartet played a soft instrumental version of "La playa," and not a single seat was left empty.

Jennifer stood before the mirror, adjusting the simple white dress that floated around her as if angels had sewn it. Not extravagant. Just... perfect. Her dark hair was swept up in soft curls. Her eyes were steady. Her smile radiated peace. She didn't walk; she floated. No tiara. No veil. Just her mother's silver watch on her wrist — ticking again, thanks to a new battery Sebastian had secretly installed. And for a moment, everyone forgot how to breathe.

When she stepped into the nave, Sebastian gasped audibly. He had seen her strong. He had seen her broken. But he had never seen her like this — glowing, ethereal, almost untouchable.

Jonas held the tiny pillow with their rings, walking solemnly like a miniature knight. And little Felipe Andrés cooed in Franz's arms, watching his mother walk toward her forever.

When the priest asked for vows, they kept it short. Jennifer looked into Sebastian's eyes and said:

"I found you when I thought I was lost. I choose you today, and I will choose you every day after."

Sebastian's voice cracked as he replied:

"You found me when I didn't even know I was looking. I am yours, now and always."

The kiss sealed it. Not as fireworks. As sunrise. Steady. Warm. Inevitable.

The ceremony was full of whispered tears and soft smiles.

Camille held Jonas on her lap, whispering translations into his ear. Katherine flew in from Barcelona, and Jennifer's sisters arrived from Colombia, bringing her father with them. Some old friends from the IMF and World Bank circles joined too, all surprised yet thrilled.

Fairfax, Virginia. Prosperity Avenue. Uscis Field Office (Today).

A year later, they sat side by side in the USCIS office on Eisenhower Avenue.

"So, this is your... fourth marriage?"

They smiled.

"Third," said Sebastian.

"Same guy," added Jennifer.

"Just... chapters," he said.

The agent raised a brow but smiled despite herself.

She flipped through the thick stack of documents.

"And the child? Jonas — is he legally in your household?"

Sebastian nodded.

"He's Camille's son, but he stays with us regularly. He has his own room. We help raise him."

The agent jotted it down.

"And your current immigration status petition includes... Luis Felipe?"

Sebastian placed a hand gently on Jennifer's.

She beamed.

"Jennifer, Luis Felipe and one more," she said, placing an ultrasound photo on the desk.

The agent looked down. Her eyes widened just slightly.

"Are you expecting?"

Jennifer nodded.

"Four months."

"Do you know the gender?"

Jennifer and Sebastian looked at each other.

And then, in sync with the kind of harmony only survivors can carry, they said:

"It's a girl, her name will be Juliana."

That afternoon, while Jennifer watered the plants and Sebastian read Jonas a story on the couch, Luis Felipe slept.

Her phone buzzed. She opened the email slowly. And then gasped. Sebastian turned.

She showed him the screen: "Status update: APPROVED. Adjustment granted. Permanent resident confirmed."

Sebastian stood, lifting Jonas in one arm and Luis Felipe in the other.

And she laughed through tears.

"It's done," she whispered.

"No," he said, pulling her in tighter. It's just beginning."

ABOUT THE AUTHOR

Luis Omar Herrera Prada is a Colombian writer passionate about storytelling that blends emotional depth, resilience, and cross-cultural journeys. Drawing inspiration from real-world struggles and second chances, he crafts stories that explore the intersection of love, memory, and identity. *Karma: All Our Chapters in Just a Second* is his debut novel.

Made in United States
North Haven, CT
02 June 2025

69430248R00098